Funeral Home

Funeral Home

BY FRANKLIN G. HEMPEL

CHAPEL HILL
PRESS, INC.

Published by The Chapel Hill Press, Inc.
1829 East Franklin Street, No. 300A
Chapel Hill, NC 27514

ISBN Number 1-880849-62-3
Library of Congress Catalog Number   2003106073

Printed in the United States of America
07 06 05 04 03   10 9 8 7 6 5 4 3 2 1

"Let us cross over the river and rest
under the shade of the trees."

LAST WORDS OF
GENERAL THOMAS JONATHAN
"STONEWALL" JACKSON

≈ 1 ≈

His name was Marcus Reel. It shouldn't have been that, but years ago, when his grandfather disembarked in Galveston, the process to shorten Rechtnagel by deletion somehow began. Marcus was never to be Markus Rechtnagel. Hard and rough and uneducated Teutonic folk, his progenitors made their way south and west about a hundred and fifty miles, secured their places as farmers and dairymen, carriage mechanics and carpenters, and every once in a while married someone who "talks that Wendish." Eventually came to be born Marcus, a few days after those whose genes he shared opened the war in Poland that the world would have to fight until exhausted. Six years of life would be bracketed by the onset and end of war before his first school year could begin a few days after Hiroshima and Nagasaki. There were fearful stories of death those days and photographs of soldiers and decapitated people and prisoners being executed that stayed with him. Coffee in silver tins tasted of wood when boiled on a sooty stove that burned coal oil, and saccharin sweetened and over-sweetened the iced tea, when tea could be found, and when his father drove the four miles over a gravel road to bring the blocks of ice home in a slow 1934 Chevrolet that had drain holes punched in the floor

1

between the seats. Hours Marcus would spend looking up as the air throbbed with flights of bombers and fighters in formation. These dark machines of the sky were so magnificent, and they were surely assigned a part in those same war books where the pictures of rubble and running people and explosions were crystallized so explicitly. San Antonio was so close, maybe fifty or sixty miles, that the air was splintered by planes just about every day. He was afraid, afraid that his father would have to go into the war and die. It never happened, and never would have, because the house on this farm, The Farm, was filled with his three brothers and three sisters and his father was too old anyway. Then the bomb was dropped on Hiroshima, and his parents spoke in low, concerned tones and issued their own fears about unthinkable weapons that now caused soldiers to drop dead everywhere with the push of a button. Their inchoate education, a total of nine years of grammar school between them, hopelessly failed them as the atom bomb came to be, and a new language of physics was required of their broken English.

The war ended, and the books of battle photographs were put away with the pictures of cousins in uniform just when the last baby was conceived. Four sons and four daughters, born in mysteriously paced two-year separations to migrants who moved from one worn-out piece of land to the next so frequently that no child was born in the same place as the one older. People would look at the boys and tell the father, "you will have a lot of help on the farm," assigning them in their very childhood to a future of farm-only labor. It seemed it would be so, always. Marcus couldn't know it, but he, now at eight years of age, wouldn't be working on The Farm much longer, and he would do little work on any other beyond then, but at that moment, there were chickens everywhere, about twelve thousand of them at a time. Baby chicks arrived in boxes divided in fourths, a comfortable, warm, syrup-smelling symphony of peeping. They were ladled onto the dried sugarcane litter by the handfuls, and the brooder canopies with their coal-oil heaters were set up to carry them through the nights of these early winter days. Heaters went out, and hundreds of the cool little orphans were picked up in the early morning. With each passing day, work grew as the chickens grew. More feed had to be hauled, more watering troughs had to be maintained, coccidiosis came along and the blood-tinged droppings meant more casualties and even fewer chickens would meet the buyer. Pipes froze, water had to be carried by hand, and each of the boys would slip socks over his hands, futile measures. One-hundred-pound sacks of feed were dragged from a donkey cart and emptied. Little boys carrying man-sized loads.

Sometimes it would be cold enough that eggs froze and burst on the kitchen counter, and the brothers pretended to be smoking in bed and blew their breath vapors into smoke rings and saw the steam rise when they pissed off the porch in morning. They mixed milk and sugar and vanilla, and put it outside to freeze. The wash pot was fired to boiling for scalding and scraping a hog, and the afternoon and evening would be filled with the motions of cutting meat, of guts being cleaned and sausages stuffed, and the wonderful smells of bony meat and organs cooking in the same wash pot for the other kind of sausage, as the cold winter day wound down. The smokehouse would be going the next day, and soon the rats would have found the bacon hanging there, gnawing holes in every other slab. Rats never seemed to bother the sausage.

Then, a spring day would come, quickly, as abruptly as those brittle cold days often came with a blue norther. Color sprang from the pastures everywhere. Bluebonnets, Indian blankets, primroses, winecups, and other blossoms of white and yellow coursed over the rises of the hills and along the fence lines, while here and there vermilion-colored sandstone rocks, eroded and pitted from some ancient force of water, interrupted and embellished this extraordinary scene. Marcus never voiced his fascination with the smells and sights of these vernal eruptions, nor did his parents ever call attention to such gentle beauty that was offered free of charge. The family knew that the hard work of the fields and the heat of the summer would begin now.

This was an interval in an early time, a kind of life to leave behind. High school was just four months past, the summer as a roustabout in the oil fields was over. Now Marcus was working on his personal formation, an ascension from the usual work in grocery stores and filling stations in the town of Guadalupe City to a level that would give him a home, decency and pride, and a grander purpose. He was smart enough to know what he needed to propel himself into a domain completely beyond where his background and status had thus far held him, what he could draw from the older ones around him. There was a beginning for him in the junior college, not much more than an extension of his senior high, and there had been part-time work in an upholstery shop that ended abruptly when the owner's son washed out of ROTC at the Aggie school and came back to town without wearing his smart khaki uniform this time.

Then a call came about a wonderful job that was to give him many gifts, a job that would help him negotiate his transition from a now-remote baseline of German-Czech-Polish farming people and address his yearning to grow in a progression that he wanted. He would be traveling now a ramp upwards without points of inflection or reversal back to some former misery.

$\backsim2\backsim$

On this early October day in southeast Texas, a cool norther was blowing, and a bright sun almost washed the color from a deep blue cloudless sky. It was generally hot this time of year, though, and while the air may have suggested winter's coming, the temperature still rose. High school football occupied the conversations among the men, except when the World Series was on and most people deserted the streets, and sat in bars and cafes to shout and drink beer. It was that kind of day. Marcus had seen it any number of times during his eighteen years as he shuffled along DeLeon Street on his way to the McCullough-Shepherd Funeral Home to see about a position there for a student. He stopped and looked into the windows of a plumbing company where someone had carefully propped up commode seats that with time had become a sad display of dust, dead moths, and flies. He recalled sitting in a school bus and seeing the same scene of neglect in another part of town, and began again his walk, forcing himself to overcome an affliction of shyness. He hated asking for a job and walked with a measured tread of fear and distress. Marcus repeated to himself the introductory sentences he would make on meeting the man to whom he had spoken a week earlier, Frank Para. Para. The name was familiar to him, the name of a seventh-grade algebra teacher whose summary punishment of serious wrongdoers was a swift crack across the hands with a ruler. Pupils were admonished aloud to brush the scum from their teeth with baking soda, and only a poor Mexican with badly decayed front teeth drew more scorn from her than the boys who rushed into class from P.E. without having combed their hair. All of the boys had ten-cent combs visibly clipped into shirt pockets or pieces of them in back pockets to allay somewhat their fears of an unkempt arrival and Mrs. Para's scathing verbal attention. This fearsome woman, who taught both a depth and a loathing of mathematics that many would carry forever, was the wife of Para's cousin, as Marcus would later learn.

Marcus continued his journey through the flat downtown, intersecting those streets named in sequence for rivers, starting with Red River at the north and ending with Rio Grande as he walked south. He moved over to River Street, and paused, gazing ahead to where it sloped off toward the south, past the Catholic girls' school, a tortilla factory, and a combination of small white houses with tin roofs and grocery stores identified both by small letters on soft-drink signs and by broad screen-door handles that advertised Butter Krust bread. An uneven brick sidewalk marked the limits of the street, and pecan and live oak trees alive with sparrows lined both sides. About a half mile further, River Street ended at the Guadalupe River, The River, with a junk-car lot on one side and a feed store on the other. Now the north wind stirred again, moving wisps of sand at the curb and causing a paper cup discarded there to rock back and forth impatiently. Sounds of playing children and dogs barking waxed and waned from the side streets.

How had he ended up here, anyhow? John brought him. It was late in the year, the middle of his fifth grade, ten years old. Motherless. There had been no birthday recognition, no Christmas, no tree, nothing for a couple of years. Now his smile had a chip in it, after a little brother unintentionally hit him in the mouth with the metal tip of a cowboy belt and broke an incisor diagonally. John, a new face, brought a truck from a feed store in Guadalupe City, and Marcus would live in that town now. John, unknowing, was the first element to represent this new life, an introduction to what might be and what might become. He wore clean, starched khaki clothes and smoked a cigar in a holder with a gold band. There was a slightly perfumed smell from the pomade in his hair, and an attitude of quiet earnestness as he helped load, wearing leather gloves, speaking in short sentences only when addressed. Marcus sat between the driver and two brothers as John urged the old truck south, groaning and grinding up the switchbacks of the green bluff, past the monument to those Texas heroes who drew the black beans from among the white ones and were executed by the Mexicans, and gaining speed that he could appreciate by looking at the highway through the hole where the gear shift stood. He was flying now, or so he thought.

The rolling hills and pines and dairy farms gave way gradually to a flat landscape of long vistas and a bowl of a sky filled with cumulus clouds. Pastures with knots of deep green live-oak trees, and mesquite and huisache, and sleek black cattle, a new kind, became common. Flocks of snow-white cattle egrets rose and rotated and settled among the grazing animals, but Marcus didn't know what they were. He asked John, " What kind of birds are those?" He thought John said "Eagles," and dozed off.

They came into Guadalupe City, passed the sign of The Oasis, painted in big block letters on the green roof of a beer joint beside a railroad spur that carried the extraction from a deep and long gravel pit behind it, and turned onto a narrow street that first bisected two cemeteries and then entered the city park, tracking The River as it wound back and forth.

They drove where people lived, with palm trees and banana trees in the yards of pleasant white frame homes at first, and further on, to magnificent and old, brilliant white homes with expansive yards and massive live oaks, and white columns and porticos and flat lawns of deep, deep green. What homes they were! Surrounded by their stone walls covered with vines, their strong wrought-iron gates served to deflect the poor whites, or Mexicans, or Negroes, or anybody unlike the occupants within. Mansions, block after block, magnificent places, and streets with names spelled out in blue and white tiles on the curbsides. What a wonderful introduction to a new hometown. Then, coasting downhill, the truck crossed The River. Marcus would be living "across The River." Here, there were no fine homes and fine families of oil wealth and income from vast ranches and rice farms. Here lived poor men who came home drunk and awakened at mid-day to piss, weaving, off the porch in front of their neighbors, and their screeching wives, and their too-young daughters who wore makeup and looked like whores, and their unwashed sons who dropped out of junior high and got jobs anywhere and in any way. Here boys with BB guns popped the silky and dignified cedar waxwings that lit in the chinaberry trees, and the robins, and ate the robins. And The River, bringing a waist-deep flood of café-au-lait water every year or two, hated that part of town.

John pulled off the highway, traveled a few hundred feet, and pulled into the yard of a distressed and abandoned house, overgrown with bush-es and tangled brush. This was impossible. After all, farther down the street were rows of little houses, simple rectangular boxes standing on cement blocks a foot or two above the ground, but covered with white asbestos siding and looking like, more or less, presentable family homes. The house Marcus saw from the cab of the idling truck was clearly not meant for people to live in. It had the unfinished look of an old shed, sagged here and there, and the floor of the porch together with the floor of the front room formed a continuum with the color of the dirt in the yard. There was an upstairs, never painted, of small spaces with pitched, sloping ceilings, reached via a steep incline of steps, where most would sleep. The father of Marcus and his new wife and her fretful baby and two of her four children would sleep downstairs near the front door, with a lit-tle sister and her stepsister in a bed nearby.

The family downstairs had the luxury of the only source of heat, a tin woodstove whose weak fire did little for the rest of the house. A small elec-tric stove, one burner working and the other rusted and useless, identified the kitchen. Water was carried in from a hand pump, just to the right of the outhouse in the backyard.

The father Reel and his new family, having traveled ahead in the red, windowless panel truck that he had borrowed from his new job, began

unloading the barrels and boxes that his bride had used for her possessions. The beds having been set up and a few utensils found, the group
had a supper of oatmeal with evaporated milk and tried to sleep, hearing
soon from downstairs the monotonous creaking as marital hormones
required action. In the morning, there was a hole in the oatmeal box, and
the rat droppings were picked out before the oatmeal was cooked. It was
the same the next morning and the next. The father asked for and found
an old .22 without a stock at his feed-store job, and wielding it like a pistol, shot at the rats each night. All enjoyed this game and kept a tally of the
numbers of rats he bagged. Sneaking into the kitchen, he would snap on
the light and fire away with rat-shot as the rats scurried up and down the
naked studs of the wall, occasionally knocking one, twitching agonally, to
the floor. Those floors, caked and caulked with dirt, had seldom been
cleaned before and were not likely to be scrubbed anytime soon, even
when the bloodstains of fallen murine guests began to accumulate.

The improbable marriage quickly came undone. The bed no longer
squeaked at night, and the days were filled with accusations and argu-
ments between the father and his young wife, and his loud voice raked
her: "I told you not to put those shitty diapers under the bed," and "you
don't do a goddamned thing all day but sit on your ass and smoke cigarettes." Just as quickly as she had joined, she left, and all were told, went
down to The Valley, leaving behind a few mismatched and pathetic clothes
in her wooden barrels. And the father, already a man of brutish tempera-
ment, whose summary administration of punishment had always been
with a sweat-hardened leather belt, even for the most minor offense, grew
more angry, and took to beating his children with renewed vigor.

Then a note was sent home with a little brother. "Please do not let him
return to school until he has been given a bath and some clean clothes."
Marcus brought a washtub into the kitchen, and needing it just as badly
himself, helped his sad little brother wash up before school. A tracheotomy
scar, dreadful evidence of his brother's babyhood diphtheria and his near
death, shone white and raised from the brown, dirt-mottled skin of his face
and throat. The school bus picked them up out front, on Parsifal Street,

and going back and forth in the neighborhood, gathered the kids for the trip to town. Streets, as if some cruel joke had been planned for that lesion across The River, were named for impressive Wagnerian characters: Siegfried, Isolde, Valkyrie, Brunhild. Of course, none could know the origins of these complicated names, nor did anyone have knowledge to share of such lofty artistic compositions. Then, even the school bus didn't want Marcus and his sibs, bathed or not. A decision had been made by the superintendent of schools that "home" was just beyond the range for a free ride to school and that each must pay five cents a day. The father argued in person with the superintendent, claiming, having measured the mileage in that red panel truck from the feed store, that "home" was one-tenth of a mile inside the limit. The fight continued, and one morning the five stood there—each with a potted-meat sandwich wrapped in used wax paper or a wrinkled bread bag—cold and hardly filled with oatmeal and diluted evaporated milk, and watched the bus speed past. They went back inside and ate their sandwiches and waited for a supper of too little.

There wasn't enough money coming in from his father's job at the feed store, and most likely, he was having to use food money to get himself extricated from his odious marriage and to maintain a store of Camels for a two-pack-daily habit. Marcus would have to work during school hours. The father arranged work for him, and for one to two weeks at a time, the two would travel to farms where Marcus would catch hens, strap them to a table, and draw a blood sample from a wing vein to test for disease. Then the father got sick and lay in the front room, feverish and breathing with an audible crackling and rattling. "Go call a doctor," he said, and Marcus went to the Mahalics' across the street, only to hear Mrs. Mahalic's puzzled exclamations in Czech. "Damn Bohemians," he said to himself, and went to the shiny aluminum trailer-house parked in the middle of a gravel lot a little further down. A young woman, not unlike his former stepmother, answered his knock wearing only a soiled brassiere and skirt, a short cigarette in her mouth, her head tilted and her face drawn into a strained grimace as the rising smoke burned her eyes. Marcus explained the situation. "We don't have a phone," she said and offered to go find one. She grabbed a coat, covered her bosom, and they called from a neighbor's house. Marcus got the woodstove burning again, and put a pan of water, as instructed, on top. Not long afterward, the doctor arrived, and in the dim light, attended the sick man, gave him a penicillin injection, washed his hands, and left. The pneumonia began to clear the next day, and the father coughed up obscene yellow lumps that he spat into a dirt-filled coffee can beside the bed. The boys had to cook for him. Now, though, the extra chicken-catching money fortified them and it, together with the income from a brother's after-school job at the gas station up on the highway, allowed all of them to graduate from potted-meat sandwiches to the wonderful smells of fried summer sausage throughout the house and occasional R.C. Colas to wash it down.

The chipped front tooth became abscessed again, only it didn't pop and relieve itself in a salty flow of pus and blood as before. It got worse, and Marcus' upper gum and the roof of his mouth became purple, swollen and throbbing. His fever grew. He complained of the pain again, the father gave him an aspirin again, and told him to rinse his mouth with hot saltwater, again. Finally, he took Marcus to a dentist, early on an overcast humid morning, and they sat in the dark corridor outside the office to wait for it to open. The old dentist came in, scowled, and proceeded to get his materials ready without speaking. He was missing the pointing finger from his right hand, having had that amputated because years of holding X-ray films in place in his patients' mouths had killed it. He took a look, told the father that he would not use a local anesthetic because he didn't trust it with a young person, and with his left hand to Marcus' forehead, pinned him to the headrest, grabbed an instrument and summarily pulled what would have been a beautiful adult tooth with his four-fingered hand. Adding a look of disdain and indifference to the boy's whimpering and irreplaceable loss, he raised the lid of a trashcan and dropped the fractured incisor from sight, forever. The father paid the four-fingered dentist with begrudging motions and sniffs that wordlessly restated how the bleeding boy had inconveniently cost him money.

≈ 3 ≈

On the southwestern corner of Rio Grande and River, the funeral home stood. Marcus could see it now, and he studied it, bright white in the sun. The funeral home looked like any traditional old Victorian home, two floors and an attic topped off with a black gabled roof. A solitary lightning rod remained on one of the gables. A green, semi-cylindrical awning covered the sidewalk from the front door to River Street, and a shorter one faced south toward an opulent home that belonged to a Mrs. Buchanan. On the front lawn, on either side of the awning, tall palm trees flapped and rasped in the October breeze. Spongy carpet grass as green as the awnings blanketed the yard, and a silvery gray sign with a shaded light above identified the place.

Marcus walked up and let himself in. It was cool and momentarily very dark, in contrast to the brilliant outdoors, and smelled of cigars. Para greeted him.

"My name is Marcus Reel. I called you about working here."

Without removing a big cigar and without opening his jaw, Para mumbled his name in return and shook hands. They walked into the office. A TV set was on, and two men lay back in differing postures before it, watching the World Series. The men looked up once, but generally took no notice. Para sat behind a desk backed into a bay window on the far side of the room and placed his well-chewed cigar, long since dead, into an ashtray. He spat into a wastebasket and talked about the job. Marcus listened and glanced out the window behind Para, toward Mrs. Buchanan's, as he talked. Para had a humorless, somewhat ashen face that amplified the tiny red veins around his nose, brown horn-rimmed glasses with slightly tinted rose lenses, and a lower lip that was perpetually tucked under or missing entirely. Even without the cigar, his enunciation sounded sometimes like a dull grunt as he told Marcus that the job paid twenty-five dollars a week and that he could leave the home every other night for a date or something and take off during the day on alternate Sundays. He didn't need to wear a suit unless there was a body in the house; otherwise, he could wear work clothes for the other jobs that needed doing. Student employees put the tents up in the cemetery, cleaned the funeral home, and washed the cars, and made emergency ambulance runs and body calls. They drove in the funeral processions, helped with caskets and embalming and dressing the bodies. They lived in the funeral home and took care of things.

Para took Marcus upstairs and showed him around. One room had three single beds. Two were used by the college students. Para lived in a separate room with a dresser and some simple accessories.

"That would be your bed there," and he pointed to one set in a bay window just above the similar window that the pair had left downstairs. Marcus would be glad to sleep in such a comfortable corner, able to see the rich lady's house next door, and slightly away from the others. They walked down the hall to the preparation room. It had a chemical smell, not unpleasant. The walls were painted a glossy white, made even more antiseptic by a bank of fluorescent lights overhead. An enameled white table a little longer than a human body stood in the center of the room. It was mounted on a pedestal and tilted toward the foot to drain into a big laundry sink. He thought that the trough around the periphery of the table would surely flow with blood during the embalming process. Above

13

the foot of the table was a pump for injecting the embalming fluid. It had a glass reservoir, open at the top, and a base from which two tubes, leading to the table and the dead, emerged. Neat rows of orange and pink bottles of embalming fluid, some labeled "Male" and others "Female," were lined up on shelves in the corner. Bottles of pale-blue cavity fluid and boxes of anhydrous paraformaldehyde with the brand name "SAFE" were stacked alongside. In the opposite corner was a cabinet full of various probes, scissors and gleaming embalming instruments laid out on blue drapes. Para's work area was clean and orderly. His whole bearing was well groomed. Marcus noticed the starched white shirt, with an "FP" monogram, and an expensive tie. "Cut those lights off," he said, leading the way.

Across the hall they entered the lavender-walled casket-selection rooms. Caskets in the first group were simple in design and embellishment, usually covered in gray felt with a shallow embossed pattern, and their prices, in cut-out chrome figures atop each unit, indicated that this room was where cheaper funerals could be bought. In the second room, the caskets clearly were meant for the costlier funerals. Those who rested in these would have a silky interior and a bronze or metallic-gray case to see them on their way. The rooms had a faint pine smell, an odorant complementary to the pastel turquoise drapes covering the windows and the pale blues of the biers that held the caskets. Rosy floor lamps provided just enough light to be useful.

The upstairs was serviced by a manually operated elevator that was raised and lowered by pulling on an endless thick loop of rope that drove a large diameter sheave above it and powered the winch lines that suspended the car. It was just big enough inside for a body on a cot, or a casket box stood on end, and two passengers. Para demonstrated the system.

"You don't use the elevator when people are here for a viewing or service, because the bumping and noises of our lift can be heard out front."

They returned to the office downstairs. Para introduced him to the two men watching TV.

"This is Arthur Shepherd, and that old fart is Jack McCullough."

So these were the owners. "Art," said Shepherd, and extended his hand. McCullough, stretched out behind the desk, said simply, "Hi," and turned back to the ball game. Art wasn't very tall; he had a face full and round, dominated by thick, wet-looking lips of the kind that the kids in high school referred to derisively as gizzard-lipped. He was smoking a filter-tipped cigarette, exuding a gentleman's look with his gray suit and its silvery sheen.

Jack exclaimed, "That sombitch couldn't hit a bull in the ass with a bass fiddle!"

He, too, looked prosperous, a somewhat thin man, hair thinned out on top, with a red complexion and an old man's glasses that had gold rims around the bottom of the lens, solid and black at the top. Marcus laughed out loud at the remark. The three men smiled a little. They like me, he thought. He was home here.

"Can you start this week?" Para asked.

"Yeah, sure. I can be here after classes tomorrow, around 3:30 or 4:00."

So, Frank ran the funeral home. He was the boss man. He had just offered Marcus the job.

4

Marcus returned to the funeral home with his simple belongings stuffed into a cardboard box, his only suit folded on top, a heavy woolen black one, too hot for the climate, from J.C. Penney's. Now, he could look around. Across from the office was the chapel, a warm, ecclesiastical room with about eight rows of deep-brown pews, a backdrop of velvet mahogany drapes, and a center area where the casket stood, bracketed by bowl-shaped floor lamps that cast pink light toward the ceiling. The classical picture of the idealized, handsome Jesus hung prominently above the little organ in the corner. To the left, shielded by white latticework, was a family area, entered from the second door of the main chapel, opposite the organ. Another small chapel lay off the back hall, near the south entrance, where the family cars were unloaded. Beyond the restrooms, in a small, unfinished room, were two ceiling-high air-conditioner units, plumbed to a water-cooling tower outside. They were the source of the throbbing that Marcus heard; these were cherished machines that could beat back the humid summer. Marcus went in, disturbing a man who slept in front of a small television tuned to a soap opera, his head sideways on his hand, propped on the arm of an old stuffed chair. He stirred, exhaling aloud, rubbing his bristly head, eyes red and coming alive. Marcus explained his unintended interruption with "I'm new here."

"My name is Fernis Wilson. Everybody calls me Willie. I'm the main-*tain*-ance man," he said, emphasizing the second syllable of his title, smiling broadly and rising from his chair.

"Fernis?" Marcus asked.

"Like a stove. Mama named me, she said, after going through a Sears and Roebuck catalogue."

"Furnace" Wilson's handshake was rough and strong. He placed a smooth gray hat with a satin band, brim formed up into a saucer shape, on his head.

"That's some hat," Marcus said.

"It's a Borsalino. Mister Arthur gave it to me. No Niggeroes and damn few white folks wear hats like these."

Marcus liked this friendly soul immediately.

"Here, let me show what we need to do outside—that is, if you're ready to go to work," he said politely, and led the way with a long yawn to the garage and into a small room alongside a red panel truck, outfitted with red lights and a siren for use as an ambulance, and two heavy Cadillac funeral coaches. Here the tents and lowering devices were stored together with stacks of green, grassy carpet pieces that were used to mask the pile of dirt beside the grave and soften the image, somewhat, of the edges of that rectangular hole cut into the earth for the person who would rest there. Willie brought the pickup around to the garage door. Tents, poles, straps, simulated grass were loaded, and finally, the lowering device, a windup machine of sleek chrome beauty that would gently, quietly, slowly drop the casket forever into its place, becoming the last servant of the dead and the facilitator, an impersonal steel worker that carried loved beings from their physical representation in life and death into the memories of those who stood graveside and heard the faint singing whine of its gears.

Dietz came out then. Walter he was named, Walter Dietzel. Thin and withered, around seventy, he had seen many hundreds of the dead. His most comical feature was a scrawny neck inside a stiff, white shirt collar that had belonged to him as a much younger man. Now, his head rotated within this loop without touching, in a mechanical way like a ventriloquist's puppet. Dietz smoked with slow movements, as if each puff required thought. He watched Willie and Marcus load without assisting, mentally checking off each piece of gear as it went onboard, and they drove to Catholic Cemetery Number Two. The three of them watched Mora and his son, back to back, their shoulders just at ground level, shoveling dirt from the grave.

"What are you studying at college, Slim?" Dietz asked.

"Physics."

"Physics? Hot damn!" When they had dug down about five feet, Dietz looked into the hole and stopped them.

"We have to get this grave open, Mora. We need to set the tent up. The funeral is in just two hours. Just trim it up and leave it. McCullough raised sand with me once this month already because we were late getting ready over in that little cemetery in La Mesa. They had to hold the people in the driveway while we finished. That grave was barely three and a half, maybe four feet deep." Dietz watched the digging intently, alternately hooking his thumbs under his suspenders and snapping first one, then the other.

The men turned to their shovels, tossed the last of the black soil to the pile and climbed out, brushing their clothing, and accepted a check from Dietz with a friendly "*Gracias.*" Willie and Marcus unloaded the wooden casket box from the pickup, and lowered it into the grave, an altogether sweet pine smell added to that of fresh earth, and laid the lid at the back of the dirt. The tent was positioned and staked; the plastic grass carpeted the ground under it. Folding chairs were arranged in three short rows, the lowering device was assembled, its mainspring wound up, and it was draped to hide the hole. A final covering of grass hid the dirt. Dietz lit a cigarette and took a survey of the scene, found it complete, then said, "Let's go back. Stop at the filling station, Willie."

Willie stayed in the truck. He handed Marcus a quarter for a pack of Luckies. Dietz had given Marcus his nickname, Slim, and Marcus had observed so soon that good Willie wouldn't, or couldn't, go into certain stores.

A funeral service, and Marcus, the new man, understood that his role would be played out in the cemetery and he didn't have to wear a suit. The flowers from the chapel were rushed out of the back door to the pickup as the casket was carried under the green awning to River Street and rolled into the open coach. Family cars began loading. Willie drove fast. The three arranged the flowerpots and sprays and moved the pickup a short distance away. Dietz stood near the gravesite as the cars pulled near, caught Para's eye, pointed, and thus signed that the man being laid to rest would be carried head first. Marcus participated in his inaugural interment, and he would bury half a thousand before age twenty.

Back at the funeral home, Marcus was approached by the pale, slumping man with shallow pimple scars along his cheek bones. He had seen him at the cemetery, working, moving briskly as if there were a need to hurry.

"Hey, Marcus, I'm Russell Snow. Around here they keep calling me Hank because, I guess, I'm from Nueces and I listened to country music when I first moved in. I've just gotten back from Houston, where I took a week's refresher course. We made a body call while you were at the cemetery, and I'm going upstairs now to get started with embalming her."

Hank was the technical master, having been taught the anatomy of embalming and the psychology of funeral service at institutions with hyphenated names in Dallas and Houston. Para, Jack, and Arthur learned embalming with gravity-fed perfusion equipment from an old man who ran the Ryan Burial Service a long time before, and their licensure as funeral directors was grandfathered in as simply as getting a driver's permit. On the table was an elderly lady, and uncovered, she presented a new experience for Marcus, who had not looked upon a naked woman and before had only seen his cousin's poor black-and-white prints of nude German girls, legs spread. He acted with nonchalance, portrayed this as an everyday thing for him, used careful elocution and measured sentences with Hank, thus not to reveal the truth of his virgin's sight and the cause of his distraction.

Hank's narration as he worked was both apostolic and pedantic.

"First, we position the head on this rubber block, tilted a little toward her right. It gives the impression of a more restful pose. I place a little piece of paper towel under each eyelid and pull the lid down completely. It stays. There are commercial inserts that do this job, but they aren't necessary. Mostly, the eyelids should be closed properly. One embalmer I knew, Clint, pulled the lower lid up, and made people look like they were squinting into a bright light. Really funny. We laughed at him all the time. I close the lips with a suture looped through top and bottom on the inside of the mouth. If it's a baby, I don't close the mouth that way. Babies sleep with their mouths open. Looks natural just to close the lips a little. We raise the carotid, then the jugular. Empty three bottles of "Female" embalming fluid into the reservoir there, Marcus. Now we connect the PortaBoy and begin to perfuse the carotid in a retrograde way toward the heart, draining from the jugular. These long forceps can be used to keep the flow going from the jugular. Pull these big chicken-fat clots out. Notice that we're getting some color in both sides of the face. That means that the fluid is circulating through collateral vessels, the Circle of Willis and those ways. We suture the incision now. Now, the trocar is used to aspirate the abdominal cavity, all directions. By watching what is washing into the sink, I can tell when I have removed enough of the contents from the gut and bladder. A bottle or more of abdominal fluid, in the trade we call it 'hard as a rock,' is pushed in through the trocar, again work the trocar in and out. Cover every corner. We're pretty much done."

Marcus had scarcely noticed the passage of almost two hours.

Hank continued. "We have a female attendant. We advertise that fact. We add it to the cost of the service. We have a lady who comes in and fixes the hair and a little of the makeup. Mostly, we do everything in advance, so she just has some touchup work to do. When the family has picked out a casket and brought the person's clothes in, or if they have chosen one of our gowns, we dress the body and put her in the casket. That's it."

Marcus bathed and returned to his school clothes and class assignments. Supper would be in a little while. It was beginning to be a different kind of life.

Hank walked into the bedroom, interrupting Marcus' deep concentration on a math problem. "Frank buzzed me. We have an ambulance call," he said, wiping his hands on a towel from the preparation room. "Meet him in the garage."

They pulled out quickly, and Marcus saw for the first time the little ambulance's effect on the drivers ahead of them. It was an altogether powerful experience seeing how the cars scrambled to get out of the way of the flashing red lights and siren's wailing, and he felt nervous and uneasy about what was coming, not at all like Frank, whose steady demeanor hardly changed as he piloted around one vehicle and then the other, the speedometer needle standing on sixty.

The oil field where the ambulance call ended had such a familiar smell, that same mysterious smell that Marcus and his brothers had commented about as boys when a norther brought it from the wells of the next county. At the well site they found a muddy crater and scattered pieces of the drilling rig. The patient lay on his back, conscious and suffering, and mud-covered roughnecks stood near in their uniforms of sun- and creosote-burned arms and faces, work gloves and silver safety hats, as an honor guard would assemble for a fallen soldier. Para told Marcus how he wanted the man lifted. An engineer, cleaner than the rest, rode with them to the hospital.

"What happened?" Marcus asked. Nothing appeared broken on the man; no blood had been shed.

"Damn well blew out," he said. "We were down about fifteen hundred feet when we hit artesian water. The foreman didn't pay attention, and the drilling mud was coming back soft. It wasn't thick enough. Next thing I know, the mud started spewing out of the well and directly the whole shebang went off. Gas blew out of the ground like a tornado. It didn't catch fire, though. Sure did tear things up. We were lucky." Motioning with his work-stained hands toward the cot, he finished: "I guess he has internal injuries or something."

Their mission completed, Frank backed the ambulance into the garage and instructed Marcus where to find clean sheets for the cot. "Make sure that the other cots are ready, too," he added, with a gesture toward the wall where two similar beds stood.

"So we must use those cots in the hearses, Frank? That many won't fit in the little ambulance."

"We don't call them 'hearses' any more. They are funeral coaches, and yes, we use them for routine transfers, mostly, but if we have to run a second car on an emergency, they have a siren, and the parking lights will flash red. Of course, we've had old people balk and tell us they don't want to ride in a hearse." Para smiled at the remembrance.

A funeral and an emergency ambulance run, all on the first day at his new job. Marcus knew now that he was going to be exposed to a far more complex world than he had ever imagined.

The day drifted away, and calculus problems continued to absorb his time after supper. He slept poorly that first night, expecting something to happen. But the phone never rang.

"Let's get some coffee before you leave for class," Hank said the next morning. It was nice outside. The streets had been scoured clean by an overnight rain, and the sweet air was damp and pure. A single high bank of deep-gray clouds on the horizon, especially with the sun striking fire-red fringes above it, gave the impression of a distant mountain range, impossible for a land of such flat topography, and the tones of the sky made the funeral home even more dominant on its corner, its white board siding more intense.

A little more than a block from the funeral home, The Texas Star Café occupied a small division of Main Street, conjoined at one shared wall with the hardware store. A couple of clothing stores, a jewelry store next door, and a delicatessen completed that end of the street. It was a typical kind of diner, with its lunch counter along one side, Formica tables and booths, and the smell of coffee and frying bacon, soon to be augmented by frying hamburgers.

"Doris, this is Marcus. We're calling him 'Slim.' That's her sister, Shirley, over there," he added.

"Hi."

Marcus looked into the beautiful blue eyes of a woman not much older than he. She was beautiful all over, slim and taller than most. He watched her, noticed her breasts as she moved around, talking to customers, handling orders, smiling generously. Faint perfume came from the pink uniform she wore, from her light brown hair and body. The scent was sustained on the coffee cup that she handed him, it seemed.

She also wore a wedding ring.

"Well, how do you like it so far at McCullough-Shepherd?" Hank asked.

"I like it a lot. Para might be rough to deal with, though. He sometimes acts like somebody just hit him in the mouth with a wet dishrag."

"Oh, don't mind him. He's just a grouchy old bachelor. Most likely, he'll be one to the end of his days, even though he has a lady friend that he sees once in a while."

"Yeah, I expect so."

"What about your family, Marcus? Your parents live around here?"

"Just my dad. My mom died when I was eight. I have three brothers and two sisters here in Guadalupe City, still. We were eight kids."

"Big family. Do you see each other very often?"

"Pretty seldom. We all go our separate ways."

Hank changed the subject. "By the way, we had an interesting call at noon one day last week, Frank and I. We went to this wreck over on Navarro and took this couple to the emergency room at Moody. This guy was a lot more agitated than he should have been when we asked his name and address and the name of the woman with him. The first thing he wanted to know was whether we needed her name, too. We said we did because we would be sending a bill. Well, you know what had happened. He was out fooling around with this woman during the middle of the day, and got caught, like a rat in a trap. Poor bastard. He had a lot of explaining to do when his wife found out."

"You can bet on it."

At the grill, Shirley's husband cursed aloud as he emptied the crumb tray from the toaster. "Goddamned roaches get into everything."

"Remind me never to eat here, Hank," Marcus said, shaking his head without conviction as they left. He stole a quick glance at Doris, who didn't look up.

⇒ 5 ⇐

The changing autumn continued its transit with thin high clouds now that rendered those first November skies pale and monochromatic, much as the land, save for a bright maple or oak here and there that broke the otherwise vapid colorlessness of Guadalupe City. Marcus had found a comfortable richness in his job, in the repetitions and rhythms that he established in the funeral home: college classes that ended at noon some days; simple weekday meals at Smith's Boarding House, ten blocks distant; ambulance calls; bodies picked up; funerals. He found new friends, closer than any before, among those who worked and lived there and felt young and protected by the senior men, brotherly toward his peers. He learned more especially about the life of Dietz, the old man of the funeral home, and listened closely to the details of his stories that used, as a temporal reference, some long-ago surgery. Dietz would add "before my operation" or "after my operation" to let Marcus or Willie or Frank know just when a particular event took place.

Marcus began to observe how the life of one human ends and the life of the other goes on. Moreover, he identified, in the people who came in and out under the long green awning out front, some internal core formed somewhere and at some time when souls have touched and a message is left with the living, maybe as unrecognized as the insensate sweat on cool skin. Other times, the journey of one's life had, with all its biting disappointments and soaring triumphs, handed over its value to the survivors with diamond clarity. Now, too, he appreciated how his own indeterminate upbringing had bred many talents and how the vagabond and unhappy restlessness in himself had sharpened his observations so that he could comprehend the meaning of a life he had seen die and also understand the sorrow of those close to the dead.

Saturday. The house was empty and the morning was passing with pedestrian dullness. The office was quiet. Para's brother walked in from the blacksmith shop across the street, extended a white hand, and sat down. He was a gentleman, a farmer who always wore gloves at work and never had the usual cracks and calluses expected of one who customarily used the rough implements of agriculture. Once he was a post office employee, and gossip had it that he discovered a knack for feeling money in letters and that he had exercised his talent from time to time, until he was caught and received a short prison term. He came out, married a schoolteacher, and kept his hands as soft and sensitive as a woman's cheek, as if he expected the ability to detect a few bills in an envelope to come in handy again someday. He often talked about the weather and found like and enthusiastic replies in the funeral home.

McCullough leaned back in the office chair, feet on his desk, reading the morning paper, checking the obituary column for typos in those announcements of the previous funeral and for business that may have gone to the competition. "Joe has a baby," he said, to anyone listening, seeing a notice from the Conner Mortuary. McCullough was in a glum mood. Jack, Jr., had his picture in the sports section, with a caption identifying him as the head cheerleader at Guadalupe City High School.

"Just what I've always wanted," McCullough grumbled, "a son who's head cheerleader." Jack, Jr., was a sissy, but no one said it out loud. Hank started making exaggerated gestures, a limp-wristed pantomime, rolling his eyes up and lifting his head like Mae West used to do. McCullough, hidden behind the paper, strained to pass gas, got up, snapped his hat on, and said, "I'm going to check out the snatch at the Texas Star," referring to the female apparatus with that word, and they watched him walk smartly across the street to Connell's blacksmith shop. He shouted to Wayne, the handyman, good-naturedly, ending with an echoing pronouncement, "You know you fellows like one thing better than watermelon." Everybody on the street could have heard his second word for a woman's genitalia, even in the parking lot of City Hall, but McCullough could care less. It was his outrageous procedure, obscene, funny, tinged with the insincere malice of older people. McCullough was in a better mood now.

Willie, Hank, Dietz, and Marcus started a domino game in the garage. "Tell me, Willie," Marcus asked, "is it true that colored people had to ask for *Mr.* Prince Albert because it has a white man's picture on the can?"

"I don't know 'bout that," he responded, "because we always called it 'Mr. Prince Albert.' Do you know that a can saved my life one time? It was in my shirt pocket, and this man tried to stab me down on The Lane, and that knife went right through that can and barely cut me."

No one could be sure of the veracity of that story because Willie always smoked Luckies, but it was an entertaining anecdote. McCullough came in, and took Hank's place. He played fast and free, scoring multiples of fives with practiced smoothness and finesse, rapping the board with his chalk scores, opening and closing his stories of sex and debauchery, his misspent youth and reckless early years as a funeral director, when he had used a bed in the back to service the married receptionist, a bed nominally reserved for the occasional woman who fainted during a particularly poignant and overwhelming funeral. Willie chided him for a mistake, became flippant. The game ran its course, McCullough got up. "I'm going to have to quit playing dominoes with Willie. He's getting too goddamned familiar." Willie heard, sucked air through his front teeth, first one side, then the other, rubbed the balding ridges above his forehead, looked at McCullough and into the sunshine out the garage door, his facial expression reminding Marcus so much of George Stevens when the Kingfish had crossed Sapphire. McCullough was in a bad mood again.

The next week, the four played dominoes as before, and the jokes and jibes came from McCullough as fast as ever, and Willie's loud, genuine laughs carried through the back, and he rubbed his head and studied his next play, arranging his dominoes, moving his lips, counting silently, bobbing his head with his calculations like a pigeon walking.

"Dietz," Marcus asked, "are you going to die this winter?"

Dietz turned, his toothless face grinning, his skinny neck on a pivot. "You smart college sonafabitch," he cackled, "I'll be there to throw dirt on your face." Willie threw his head back and laughed, a concourse of gold-capped teeth flashing in the light from the yard.

It was uncommon for someone to ring the doorbell in the middle of the day. Standing there in a chocolate-brown suit was a thin man with an absurdly narrow face and Brylcreem-greased hair combed flat and cleanly parted. The first thing Marcus noted was his eyes, one brown, one gray, as if nature didn't quite get the matched set. He extended his hand and spoke in the words and accent of a poor east-Texas education, "I'm Jimmy Hoff, and I'm here to see about a job. I'm working at a funeral home in Galveston now, and this place looked pretty darn good when we came here to pick up a body a few months ago."

Marcus didn't remember him, and doubted his story, but asked him to come into the office. He called upstairs to Para on the intercom. "Frank, there's a man down here asking about a job."

Jimmy was the rare non-student brought on board. He moved in, and followed Marcus like a lost lamb. After Marcus bought a pipe, Jimmy bought a bigger one with a bowl that blocked out his too-small face and puffed confidently, surrounding himself in a vanilla-scented cloud of London Dock. He often repeated tales about the conditions of crashed cars and their bleeding and broken occupants, as well as other stories of a night's work, and made unearned assumptions about his importance in handling the persons at an accident. Here was a man of little physical quality—decent, though, in his intentions—but Jimmy's egotism was annoying, and only his unlettered naiveté made his weak arrogance tolerable. Still, he was a friend that Marcus could count on to give up his last dollar and share with him the wisdom that comes with survival in an indifferent world. Moreover, he willingly jumped in on emergency calls in the middle of the night with an uncommon alacrity.

The phone call at midnight was like a facial slap that awakened the sleeping men. It was a rare night that Frank was spending on vacation elsewhere. Hank turned on the bedside lamp, took the details. "You awake, Reel?" he asked, looking over as he hung up.

"I'll go with him," Jimmy volunteered.

"No. I have to go. There's been a death most likely. You couldn't bring the body in. You have to be a funeral director for that."

Marcus got into the ambulance with Hank, and they sped away to the northeast. Maybe it was the clarity of the winter night on the flat, straight road between the rice fields that made the plaintive sound from the wrecked car so poignant. Music surrounded them in the night, "The Trumpeter's Lullaby" playing on the radio, flowing through the broken windows and out of the hole where the windshield had been. A few silent people and the authorities were there, holding flashlights, a spontaneous vigil for a young man who would never hear another pleasant melody. They pulled him from beneath the dashboard and laid him on the cot as the lullaby ended; then the radio died during the announcement, "Clear-Channel Station KVOO, Tulsa."

Jimmy stepped into the pure white light of the preparation room. "Do you know this boy?"

"Yes, I do," Marcus answered. "I went to school with him. The highway patrol told us at the wreck who he was."

"Yes, it's Raymond Haschke. What a shame." Marcus looked at the fractured body, the long hair standing up, blue jeans bloodied and torn, and now identified the familiar features of the first friend he had made upon arriving in Guadalupe City and entering the fifth grade. Death and the missing eyeglasses had at first made the face of his old classmate foreign.

Jimmy noticed the reaction on Marcus' face. "I'm really sorry, Slim."

Marcus was glad that he didn't remember the last time he saw Raymond. It would be too sad, knowing that such an instant would end their earthly friendship, that eternity would be its future. Better to have lost a friend and have no recollection of the last conversation, the final visual image, than to say goodbye to someone for what you knew to be the last time.

In the cemetery, Marcus stood near the men of the family, a circle of somber faces, gathering to return to the family cars. He knew the father, the owner of a furniture store, who spoke: "I always tell Mama that a good stew has to have meat with the bones on it. Short ribs, or chuck roast, something like that. The bones give it the flavor. No, she always wants to use stew meat without the bones." The man stopped talking. His lapse from that moment in time, from its cruel reality, for a simple conversation about a trivial daily food, ended, jerked up short. He felt again the black pain that poured over him and the others like a wet, cold mass of something liquid, and he stared at the ground with watery eyes. If only he could stop thinking about his son, his firstborn, who lay in the ground. If only he could understand why, why now, why didn't that boy stay at home that night? He'd be alive today.

Then the grandfather added an audible and prevalent coda: "Why couldn't it have been me? I'm old. I've lived my life. He was just beginning his."

Marcus gave himself a silent statement, final rites for his friend: "Goodbye, Ray, old buddy. I'll always remember you, running alongside your bicycle, pushing it across the school yard in the fifth grade."

He drove the family home and then returned to his.

≈6≈

"Hail Mary, full of grace; the Lord is with thee; blessed art thou amongst women, and blessed is the fruit of thy womb, Jesus." The words of the rosary being said in the chapel reached the office in a modulating volume that sounded a little like the choruses of unknown and unseen insects that swarm during summer afternoons. Marcus looked after the chapel when the last of the small crowd had left. He lowered the casket lid, turned off the lights, and locked the front door, the closing of another day. After doing some minor straightening, he went upstairs, leaving the others, including Jimmy leafing again through a limp newspaper that had passed through many hands.

Hank had sat erect behind the desk early that morning, reading aloud from that same paper. "It says here that the driver lost control of his car and crossed the center line, hitting the second car head on. Lost control, my ass. It was suicide, plain and simple." Marcus had to agree. A wreck like that between two cars on a straight road under an overcast sky, no other cars leading or following, had to be deliberate. The couple in the second car survived somehow, bearing horrific injuries to their lower legs and splattered with a macaroni salad that had been launched from

31

the rear seat. Their trip to a reunion or a church function or the home of a friend was over.

The ambulance was summoned to a flaming house around midnight, and Marcus was immediately carried back to the terrible night when his uncle's cotton shed caught fire and Marcus had struggled, with a broken back, to the porch into heat and light on that muggy summer night. The yard of this little home at the end of a gravel street, where they now arrived, was strewn with a tangle and confusion of fire hoses, and urgent, shouting men with flashlights and turning and blinking emergency lights made it clear that something bad had happened. A fireman came up to Hank and Marcus, his face oddly unrecognizable in the monochromatic red revolving light that passed across it in exact intervals. "There are two kids in there. You'd better get them out pretty quick, because the whole thing is about to collapse. We don't have enough water down here to put it out. They're toward the back. Here, I'll show you."

They followed, leaving the cot near where pieces of the front steps remained. The porch had burned away, and they jumped up on the joists like tightrope walkers and moved through the front door. The wet, smoky smell, the bitter, choking, steaming air inside was thick with tragedy. Above, the burning ceiling, blackened, reticulated like the bark of a dogwood tree, glowed and crackled with the sound of dry leaves being crushed. The fireman pointed his flashlight, the beam making a bright track through the smoke, at two forms near the back door. There, in the corner, not three feet from the back door, lay the two children. It was easy to reconstruct. They had begun running toward the back door, and had almost made it, collapsing into an offset that jutted out, where they perished and now were charred like the walls around them.

Marcus stooped to pick up the first child, but it was too hot to carry barehanded. "Hank, we'd better get the sheets off the cot," he said. He doubled a sheet and threw it over the littler person, and wrapping his hands around the bundle, lifting it up, handing it to Hank. The second child, crumpled into a ball, pressed into the corner was the larger and more difficult to move, and Marcus was reluctant to cause a limb to separate as he wedged his hands behind and underneath, discovering that it was not as hot in that sheltered spot, and he rolled the child close, hugged it to his chest and began picking his way back out of the room, balancing on the floor joists, concentrating, lest he fall with his poor little charge. Then they were on the cot, the black drape over them, and Hank and Marcus were waiting for permission to remove them when their mother skidded up, wheels scattering the gravel, a look of disbelief, almost annoyance, registering on her face.

"What happened? What happened?" she cried. "Where are my kids?"

In a monotonic, factual voice that betrayed both his deep disgust and anger with this woman and his unwillingness to break the news gently, one of the police officers said, "They burned to death, m'am."

Para came into the preparation room. Awakened from his bed, his voice still resonant with sleep's effects, he shook his head. "Get out the SAFE." Marcus had never seen such sadness in one who had embalmed so many. An ugly trickle of dark-red liquid made its way down the table, toward the hole at the end. They laid the children on plastic sheets and covered them with the powder, and wrapped, they slept as cocoons in white, powdery preservation.

The news came in bits and pieces. The mother, carhop at a drive-in, on her night off decided to leave for a while after her girls had irritated her boyfriend just by being present, and he had gone home. She followed him; they coupled and slept. Back home, perhaps from the cigarettes the lovers had left smoldering somewhere, no one knew, the fire began, and the little girls, asleep on the couch in the front room had tried to escape into the backyard. Had they gone out the front, the town may never have known of the unwise decision this wretched, uneducated woman had made that night to leave them alone. Now, at the funeral, freed of the children now lying together in a single casket as they had died, folded together, hardened sculptures like the children of Pompeii, she wept non-stop, occasionally looking upward, mouth open, displaying her decaying and missing teeth. The boyfriend, for whose maleness she had sacrificed her babies, was not among the few mourners who were there. With the cheapest of the caskets, buried in the poorest section of the cemetery, the funeral home gave her the most they could: the burden of motherhood was lifted, and she could move on, out of town, out of memories, forever.

7

Marcus began the walk up the sloping street toward the city library on a December day that brought cold, moving air of uncommon sharpness. The sky was pure majesty, a tent cover of white clouds on a blue field. From the left, a dark-haired man on crutches cut across the street diagonally and began his rhythmic driving up the sidewalk ahead, brilliant chrome crutches flashing alternately in the afternoon sun as he gained distance. Marcus knew him. It was Alvin from his high school days. Alvin always seemed angry about his thin poliomyelitic legs, a reputation that grew after an airman from the base outside of town supposedly kicked his crutches from beneath him, then had the misfortune to get so close that Alvin was able to grab a leg and drive a knife into the flyer's calf, pulling the blade in an arc through the muscle as one would cut a deep score into an orange for peeling. Marcus stayed clear of him, especially after remembering the scorn on Alvin's face when he had been allowed what was deemed unfair leeway in the chinning contest to drop less than all the way down to a point where the arms locked straight at the nadir of each repetition. With his powerful upper body that now carried him beyond the library with surprising speed, Alvin would have won against all competitors anyway. Without breaking the regular cadence of his crutches, he turned the corner and was gone.

Alvin lay on the embalming table. The bent and emaciated legs could burden him no longer. Only a small, sutured cut above his left ear, the hair around it shaved away, gave any external clue to the violence that the preparation room would transform into a kind of cosmetic peace. Through him, the phrase *subdural hematoma* was now commonplace in the newspaper of Guadalupe City. A fight, a seemingly inconsequential tap on the side of the head with an empty beer bottle, a headache, coma, death, and an arrest, all within a twenty-four-hour epoch. Marcus ushered the family into the office, watched the mother. No father appeared. He asked himself about her feelings, and saw a confusion of anger, frustration, pain, fatigue, sorrow, and sensed the long, hard life she had endured in administering to her stricken son, his infirmity, and his brutal anger.

Her screams filled the selection room when she saw the caskets. "My baby, my baby! He was such a good boy. Everybody liked him. My baby!"

Alvin was in the chapel now, his useless legs hidden under the lid of the lower half of the casket, the pink lights giving some warmth to a stony face at rest, that mean-spirited face now no more than an anonymous mannequin in death. Para brought the family in for their first look. The mother grieved convulsively and wailed, "They killed him. His hair is shaved off. He was such a good boy. They killed him. I hope they die like he did."

Alvin was gone. The screeching denunciations continued from a mother who wanted more punishment, more retribution from the scared kid from the Catholic school who had not meant to hurt Alvin or anybody when he let go with a bottle. But underneath it all, another, more demonstrative emotion appeared in the mother, a kind of disdain and relief combined, and her public and lachrymose suffering didn't seem so genuine any more. And slowly, Marcus understood. He remembered his own father's oft-spoken demand the summer after high school, "Boy, you ain't going nowhere until you pay me back for raising you." The mother wanted recompense for having raised a crippled boy who needed care. He had died abruptly, and she had not been given something she thought she deserved somehow. And so it wasn't Alvin's struggle and misfortune with his burdensome legs or even anger that fate had suffered on him the infantile paralysis in that terrible summer of 1952 when so many others fell ill. It wasn't Alvin who sounded the vitriol, nor had Marcus ever heard him raise his voice to demean or injure. It was Alvin who worked so hard at poling himself along while others walked effortlessly, whose aching pain was not diminished at all by the motor uselessness that fooled outsiders into thinking his legs and joints were numb, and it was Alvin who tried his best not to touch the ground with his withered legs as he chinned, because he did not want to appear to have an advantage, and he could not raise them, so he did not straighten his arms when he reached the bottom of his repetition. His grim face in life, cold and unsmiling, was clear to Marcus now as the only testament to the energy he had to expend, not so much to carry his half-body, as it was to live in a fatherless world with a mother who hated him.

8

Marcus arranged his tie in a Windsor knot, as Frank had taught him early on, choosing that symmetrical knot over the simpler one that required the backwards motions he used to dress dead men. He looked at himself in the mirror, giving himself approval for the new suit that he had just bought, and picked a little at the pimple that needed attention on his forehead. Now that the hair in his once-flattop cut had been allowed to grow longer, he could comb it over, and it seemed to fit the need in his mind's eye to appear older. He needed to put on some weight, though, he thought. Some muscle. Might make his frame fill in. He was eating better food now, to be sure. "How damn tall are you?" Jimmy had asked one time as they stood together. "Taller than you. That's all you need to know, man," was his quick comeback. Jimmy had pretended to choke him. "I'll take you down a notch or two," he said, as they scuffled about the bedroom.

They walked over to the Texas Star. Marcus spoke to Hank and Jimmy of his faint association in junior high with Alvin and filled in the details of Alvin's schoolyard behavior. "He always seemed so mean." He added some remarks of admiration about Alvin's strength at pushing himself uphill on crutches. Marcus didn't use the phrase, but Alvin could move with the efficiency of a coxswain's crew.

At the café door, Marcus noticed Doris approaching on Main Street.

"Go on in," he said to the others. "I'll catch up with you later."

"Hi, Doris"

"Hi."

"Where have you been?"

"The bank."

Her blue eyes fixed on him, the smile warm. Her complexion of half-cream, half-milk, backlit by the low morning sun, now seemed incandescent, and the light coming through the fenestrations of her hair gave it a peach-colored and brassy glow like sunset on high cirrus clouds in the western sky.

"Come on in. What can I get you?"

"Cherry pie and coffee."

Doris placed a brown envelope in the cash register and moved toward the pie case.

"What's the story on her, Hank?" Marcus asked.

"The way I hear it, her husband still lives in their house, but they are supposed to be separated. He takes care of the kids while she works. Why, would you like to get a little of that?"

"Well, sure."

"Too bad, Slim. You probably can't have it, not now, anyway. But you could always try *her* if you're hard up," Hank grinned and leaned over the table, gesturing with his fork toward Shirley, whose back was turned. Poor Shirley. She was the sister with the small bosom, thick legs and big backside, and a kind of mouth that, when it opened in a smile, gave her a rodent look as her upper lip pulled up.

Jimmy laughed gutturally. His brown eye reflected the sunlight from the front window more than the gray one. "Slim, your odds of getting some from Doris are about the same odds an armadillo has trying to cross the highway. All you are going to end up with is Ma Thumb and her four daughters, just like always."

"For you, Jimmy," Marcus said amusedly, giving Jimmy the finger as Doris brought the pie. "This is certainly better than a bacon grease and sugar sandwich," he murmured, looking down.

"You ate that, Slim?"

"As kids. It was about all we had sometimes."

"Hank," Jimmy asked, "how come we don't let people hold a wake in the funeral home? I heard Jack telling the people that we don't have wakes that often any more."

"We generally try to discourage them. They bring in coffee and sandwiches, talk and bullshit all night, and leave a lot of trash around, the ashtrays full. Besides, nobody really wants to sit up from two to four in the morning. The other thing, they poke around in the office, get into the desk and so on. Frank's favorite comment is, 'Who's going to sit with the body in the cemetery tomorrow night?' But if they have to hold a wake, we tell them to go ahead."

Barbara answered the ringing phone. "It's the funeral home," she said, holding the receiver out for Hank. "Frank said to get right back." They finished their coffee and hurried out of the door.

Para called impatiently to Marcus upstairs. "You ready to go yet? Let's get going on this body call."

"Be right with you. I'm getting my laundry together. Can you swing by and let me drop it off at Blue's?" They stopped at her little house on a dirt side road.

"Blue," Marcus asked, as he handed her his clothes, "is that your real name?"

"No," she answered, with a pleasant return expression on her face, appreciating his interest in a washerwoman's life. "It's Blanche."

"Blanche?"

"Yes, sir," she replied, never noticing the sly smile that Marcus stifled. Blue had a face so black and smooth that it was difficult to focus on her features.

Nothing could have prepared them for the scene out of science fiction that they found in the farmhouse. Standing around an open deep-freeze on the back porch, and looking in, were the county sheriff and a justice of the peace. Inside, her arms clasped around her knees in the comfortable posture of one sitting on a lawn, was the body of an old woman, her eyes partly open, her brittle gray hair glittering with hoarfrost. She, they found out, had been missing and was presumed, with her dementia and delusions, to have wandered off earlier in the week. Searchers found nothing as the hours passed, and she was believed lost in the brush along The River, probably dead under a tree somewhere or drowned and already located by the buzzards. It was when a daughter went to prepare a meal that the awful discovery was made. Whether the woman had crawled up deliberately or had accidentally fallen in while bent over, no one could say; they could only surmise that the lid must have somehow come down and latched. She was frozen between the packages of food. The sheriff made a half-hearted effort to dislodge her, let go, straightened up, and then tried again and a third time.

Para muttered to Marcus from the side of his mouth, "We could get this over with if that lard-assed Dutchman would just get out of the way."

"What do you boys want to do?" the JP asked. Marcus stepped forward and with the same effort that he had used thousands of times in the feed store, pulled the one-hundred-pound block up and balanced her on the edge of the freezer chest. They positioned her on her side, on the cot in the fetal position, from which she was unfolded a day later, thawed out on the embalming table.

Marcus stayed with Para as he worked. "What do you think, Frank?"

"I think she killed herself," he said. "She was kinda crazy and decided to kill herself this way. Who knows? When people freeze to death, I've been told, they feel warm and sleepy first."

Marcus had to agree with him. The old lady reached back into that part of her memory that remained, a happy core of infancy and childhood and younger days locked in a deranged elder brain, and remembered that freezing to death was a narcotizing, pleasant journey into infinity. She had these instincts to drive her and no inhibitions or cognitive blessings in her old life to dissuade her of her choice of a peaceful end. Taking a seat in the freezer, she had passed into the next world.

What was it like growing old? Is there some acrimony associated with survival? Marcus talked to Dietz about it sometimes, about the years to come. He was a kind old gentleman and benevolent. Marcus could direct irreverent, teasing statements at him or deliberately insult Dietz's pets with remarks about how a dog's next meal was it's last vomitus and receive no more than a mild reprimand from the man who loved his animals to the point of giving the dogs his last name and having headstones made for them. Questions for Willie were about the present, the immediate, here and now, about life's interactions and love-driven relationships, but in Dietz, who probably imagined his own thin body on the embalming table, Marcus hoped to look into the future.

About old age, Marcus slowly fashioned some kind of perspective, one in which he got older, and he had this vision of himself arriving at the peak of a steep hill, like the peak of a cone, and all of his friends and acquaintances have fallen away from him, have gone away. He remembers their voices and faces and the way they said things. He is left up there to keep on living, and it is lonely. He knew loneliness. He suffered from it as a boy and now. He saw a blind man once, a young blind man, talking to himself in a restaurant booth. How lonely he must have been, staring straight ahead into a gray sphere of sightlessness, with noises but no patterns and no depth.

Marcus sat now in the alcove behind the desk, his feet propped on top of the typewriter, and thought about how his life was rooted in the past, a past that had became continuous with the present. His long life ahead then would be constructed from both. He loved "Oh God Our Help in Ages Past," and felt all right about reading the Bible, taking one from the bench behind the organ because something in the minister's words from that last burial service remained with him. There the words were again, in Isaiah: "All flesh is grass, and all its beauty is like the flower of the field. The grass withers, the flower fades, when the breath of the Lord blows upon it; surely the people is grass." Wasn't it also true, Marcus believed, that "time like an everlasting stream, soon carries its sons away; they fly forgotten as a dream dies at opening day" ?

9

Hank drove to supper at Mrs. Smith's, and she, the widow who reminisced often about her dear husband, had resumed the care and feeding of her people now that the Christmas holidays were over. Marcus and Jimmy squeezed into the front seat, in the little ambulance this time, in case an emergency call came in. Marcus liked that part, taking the ambulance out to eat; it meant saving a little of his own gasoline. Intermittently, there were revelations of personal agonies for the group at the meal, sometimes because developing news of wrecks, tragedy, or death was carried by the men from the funeral home, and they revealed privileged information when asked. Or the diners themselves shared their troubles, even unspoken ones, by their actions. Now, there was more than lasagna at the table again, because an aching love affair had added a distracting mood among three people from the DuPont chemical plant outside of Guadalupe City. The stunning woman was in love with the indifferent handsome man, and another man was infatuated with her, in turn. She was fascinating to Marcus, and her deep-brown eyes with her equally dark hair, together with a distingue achieved by remarkably attentive grooming, captured him also. She was bright, an engineer. So, too, were the men. The first, the cavalier gentleman, looked a little like a movie star and football player. The second, the most intelligent conversationalist, a tall, lurching chemical engineer from Rice, towered over Marcus. The second bore down with longing, sideways glances at the pure red lips of his cherished lady while she fixed on the object of her love in complete obliviousness to the Rice Owl.

"That is some combination, Hank. I just can't figure it out," Marcus said. "Ann is wishing for Johnston, and he could care less. Meantime, poor miserable Tucker sits there with a hard-on; he would give anything to have her, and she ignores him. Why doesn't that guy want such a good-looking woman who is obviously crazy about him?"

"I think," answered Hank, " she's pretty screwed up. Has a lot of emotional problems. She sees a psychiatrist, too, they tell me. You've seen her jump up and tear outta there when something is said that upsets her. I suspect that old Jimbo has serviced her from time to time, but after that, doesn't really want her around. It works out that way sometimes. Maybe he already has a girlfriend somewhere. Now take Tucker. Probably the smartest sombitch that you will ever meet. He'll make a lot of money some day. Nice guy, too. It would help him to get laid. Might clear up those jack-off bumps on his face."

Marcus laughed at Hank's referring to acne that way, then felt again his own unfulfilled yearning for a kiss and his craving for a comely lover like the brown-haired one sitting opposite him at those evening meals.

Hank and Marcus answered the call from the police in late evening. They found the man lying in a ditch on the highway to The Valley, on his back, watching silently as the cot was brought to him, then, trembling, pulling himself aboard. At the hospital Marcus stood near as the attending physician removed the soiled shirt from the emaciated man, revealing, under the cold surgical light, four silvery, reflective round scars the size of quarters stitched across his sunken abdomen.

The doctor asked, "What caused these?"

"Machine gun bullets," the man answered, his words issued in a grunt, his voice as hot and dry as his skin.

"Machine gun bullets?"

"Uh-huh," came the reply, given with a long weary sigh of expiring air.

In an instant of shame, Marcus changed from thinking of the passenger as a decrepit alcoholic who was getting a free ride and a night in a clean bed courtesy of the public treasury. No, his logical inferences were absolutely wrong, for here was a warrior-hero whose alimentation gave him little nourishment after such cruel wounds and drastic surgery. Where had this happened, and when, and how? The questions bothered Marcus through most of the night, and in the morning he called the hospital and was told by the floor nurse that the man could have a visitor.

His jaundiced face was toward the ceiling when Marcus came in; then the man's yellowed eyes locked on the visitor, and the contrast between his haggard face and pure white pillow intensified. Marcus introduced himself and told the man where he had been found. He nodded in comprehension, and offered a handshake with his left, his right hand being infused from an intravenous bottle.

"Much obliged," he said.

"Where were you coming from?" Marcus asked.

"Corpus. I was in a Navy hospital there for a couple of days, and when they let me out, I thought I would hitch a ride to my sister's house in Fort Worth."

"What happened?" Marcus interrupted.

"Well, this guy picked me up, but I got sick to my stomach in the car after a while, and when he stopped so that I could puke, he drove away, the asshole. I don't really puke, but I gag a lot, and sometimes this bitter-tasting bile comes up, that's all. So, I started walking, and then, I guess that I must have blacked out there on the side of the road."

It was time for Marcus to ask, to get the point, to find out about the four bullet scars. "How did you get shot?" The man studied the question for a while, then looked out the window again. Did he not intend to answer? His jaw worked, and when the soldier finally spoke, his voice had taken on the timbre of his pain and horrific memories.

"Well, we were moving out one morning, our platoon. It was cold, and we were freezing our asses off with the piss-poor equipment that they gave us Marines in Korea. I had trench foot so bad I could hardly walk. We walked right into them, Chinese, and they opened up with machine guns. We were cut to pieces. Those who could fired back. I had a BAR and got off a few rounds when I heard this guy yell, "I'm hit! Help! Medic!" I recognized the guy's voice; he was a big tall mother from Michigan. He kept hollering, and I figured I should try to get to him and started crawling. I found him. His foot was almost gone, just hanging by a piece of skin. I sorta tied a bandage on it, the stump. A medic made it there, and I started to give him a hand getting the wounded guy up. He was heavy and hard to lift. I don't know what happened next, but I guess we exposed ourselves. One minute I was halfway standing up with this guy's arm around my neck, then bullets were flying, and I was knocked backwards, and everything went white. The medic and the guy from Michigan bought it, I found out later, and I was expected to die when they got me to the field hospital. I was doped up but still conscious, and the triage officer put me in that category they called 'Expectant.' Later they told me that it was supposed to mean 'Expectant to Live,' but it really means 'This poor bastard will take too much of the surgeon's time and will die anyway.'" He smiled a little. "But I kept on living, and they took out several feet of my insides and a piece of my liver and a kidney and I don't know what else. Now, I have a hard time keeping things down. I probably shouldn't drink either. But what the hell." His voice wavered, he stopped talking, then softly finished, "I was trying to help." Marcus didn't answer or react. The man turned to the window and again, tired and subdued, "I was trying to help."

Marcus, needing to talk, took a solitary walk along Juan Linn Street, then along its continuation, The Lane, to Willie's house. It wasn't that far, just about four blocks with some beer joints where a few old German men played "Shoot the Moon" at the domino tables, and about three blocks more of Negro businesses and bars. There was a wonderful smoke smell from the barbecue place at the last intersection, and a few people sat on porches or walked in the street that warm and peaceful Saturday afternoon.

Gently he rattled the screen door, soiled around the handle and at the hole in the screen where people had reached through to unhook it many times before. Velveeta came, smiling. Her palms were held out in front, fingers spread, as if to indicate the number "ten" or say, "*Stop!*" protecting the wet, purplish fingernail polish she had just applied. Her bare feet made no sound, and there, too, her nails were adorned, but the purple paint could do a little less to beautify those horny feet with their many white calluses that told of her years standing over sinks in restaurant kitchens or tending bar in the beer joints along Dutch Lane.

"Hi," she said. "Willie be in the kitchen."

The sun fell across Velveeta's arm, bringing the translucence of it into the room. Skin the color of honey, not the blonde honey in the little jars in the grocery stores, but that brown kind the bees make when they forage on mesquite blossoms, a cloudy amber that so often smelled faintly of the smoke the ranchers used to rob the hives. She continued to hold her fingers in the air, and joining the conversation, the ten little figures nodded up and down and danced like purple-capped puppets in rhythm with their mistress's voice and flashing, lively, greenish eyes. Velveeta had a new beau, yet another man, counting at least two or three husbands, in the lusty platoons who had marched through her bed. Marcus' mind strayed and seeing this woman prepare for her evening lover, remembered a woman they had picked up on The Lane, a wandering and sadly retarded reject whose years had been scarred by more than turns of the planet. Gathering her up from the sidewalk where she lay in a drunken collapse like a pile of dirty clothes and carrying her to the hospital, Marcus could see the waning of her young life and could only imagine her nights of debauchery when Jimmy, too, quickly offered corroboration by saying, "If she had as many pricks sticking out of her as she had in her, she'd look like a pincushion."

Willie's Luckies lay on the table. Marcus fingered the pack and read aloud, "LSMFT." "You know what that stands for?" He looked at Willie and glanced at Velveeta's tumbling derriere as she left the room.

Willie finally answered. "Lucky Strike Means Fine Tobacco. Right?"

"No. Loose Straps Mean Flabby Teats."

A flicker of amusement crossed Willie's sullen face, only a fleeting glint of mirth, although he had heard that schoolyard expression many times. He lit up. Marcus could see by the match light in Willie's eyes the aftereffects of Friday night's beer drinking. His mouth agape, Willie pinched his cigarette between his tongue and lower lip in that peculiar way he used when he studied his dominoes, not to let the offending smoke affect his next play. His hand turned the pack this way and that, the burning cigarette sticking out there like those quick lashes of the chameleons' tongues that snapped up insects with invisible speed along the fencing and wooden rails that fringed part of the backyard of the funeral home.

"I'm tired, Willie," Marcus began.

"Did you have a lot of calls last night?"

"No, just the usual. We went out on a wreck about seven, then picked up this guy in a ditch out on 77 around ten, ten-thirty." Marcus talked of the thin soldier and his wounds, and his premature evaluation of the man's reasons for being such a derelict, and his shame when the real story became known. "The problem is, Willie, I jump to conclusions about people too soon, then end up having to change my mind. I'm wrong about people, maybe more than once. I really don't understand much, I guess."

"Hell, Slim, you're only eighteen years old. I'm damn near forty, and I do the same thing. I know what it's like. You get up in the middle of the night and haul some drunk to the hospital. We never get paid for that, and if the guy dies, we may get to put him in our two-hundred-dollar special, or whatever the V.A. or Social Security allows. Sometimes, not even that. The funeral home doesn't make a dime."

"No, Willie, it's more than just having to get up and make an ambulance call for nothing. I don't know anything about girls, or drunks, or anything, either."

"You know a lot more than you think, Slim. You're damn smart, and the people at McCullough-Shepherd like you. Think about that for a while, and not about a lot of things you'll understand when you get older. As time goes on, you'll learn a lot about people who drink too much and work too little. Some just run out of luck. And then this guy you picked up. I reckon that since he had faced dyin' that way in Korea, dyin' ain't gonna mean that much to him any more."

Marcus could believe that, and he trusted Willie, who had wisdom to see dignity in a luckless life, who held a kind of respect for the lonely who lived in the lowest strata, the people who made a purposeful choice to be laid in graves without a single mourner as witness. Willie could put himself in the place of drunks with feelings, thoughts, and self-value. Derelict people, just getting by as if waiting for a final release from this world.

The melancholy did not lift from Marcus. "Maybe," he said, "I'm just tired of working. I went to work before I started first grade."

"Well," Willie chuckled, "as my old granddaddy used to say: 'You can get tired of workin' when you get tired of eatin'.'" Willie paused. "Don't be so damned stubborn about lettin' people help you." He yawned. "I need some aspirins," he said, pronouncing them "aspireens."

Marcus began the walk back up the low grade to the funeral home. He remembered a thin old Mexican who was hit by a car as he crossed the street on his way to mass one Sunday dawn. Both legs had been snapped below the knees, and the bones pierced the skin. Only a single police officer and the driver, standing distressed and coatless in the cool morning, were there. The man wouldn't let anyone lift him to the cot. He flopped forward, grasped the cot, and dragged himself, the bones making furrows in the dirt shoulder. He pulled himself aboard without a sound, and reaching down, pushed his fingers under the loops of his shoestrings, pulled his feet up with the rest of himself. Then he lay back and closed his eyes for the ride to the hospital. The driver retrieved his coat jacket as Marcus covered the man and returned a rosary to the quaking hands of the suffering old gentleman.

And now Marcus saw it in himself. He wouldn't be carried, couldn't allow anyone to take away the independence he had pressurized into himself, to power himself without help. He just had to be self-reliant, even if it led to the quick, mistaken analyses of other people and what went on inside their minds.

⌐10⌐

Mrs. Carter Smith didn't serve meals after noon on Saturdays, and Marcus drove alone to eat at Rip's Café, windows open to let the gentle nighttime air of a late winter day that felt like spring wash through his car. It would be a long night, and he wanted to eat well first. He loved the fried round steak that covered the plate and sometimes lapped over the edges, and the huge Latvian waitress who entertained the boys from the funeral home with friendly smiles and heavily accented jokes. "Vot do you know about dot?" she once said, hands on her hips, looking at the saucer she had dropped with the butter on it. Even Ralph Waldo Emerson was remembered, present that hard night on the wall of some bank where a neon sign blinked on and off, the tongue of a wagon snapping up and down from its pinion tether in time with the pink to blue changes of cursive words, "Hitch Your Wagon To A Star."

Marcus felt as if his ears were stopped up, the middle of the night was so quiet. A car pulling out of the parking lot made muffled, irritating pops as the tires crunched across the gravel. Noises seemed distant, as his affected hearing worked hard at listening for the train. There they were, at two o'clock in the morning, waiting outside the station, surrounded by darkness and silence, no light except for the single trapezoidal beam descending from a globe high on a telephone pole, and enough of an intermittent breeze to occasionally move the flat metal shade around the bulb sufficiently to produce a mellow ringing sound and deflect the swarms of moths circling beneath. And the moths, rising and dropping around the lamp, gave their shadows to the platform, moving dark spots that coursed in converging rows as the insects rose and fell. Inside the dim and pale green office, thermos in front of him, yawning as widely as Marcus and Hank, the station agent sat at his desk. The freight train was now two hours late.

The train carrying two body containers arrived, now early on a Sunday morning, and the cargo was at last with them in the garage, no more than sheet-metal boxes, handmade and crudely soldered together. Jimmy and Marcus brought two caskets down from the selection room, stripped the excelsior and fabric from the first casket and maneuvered to get the body carrier in. It was at least eight inches too long. Para examined the sheet-metal boxes, and shook his head. "Oh, Lord," he said. "We don't have oversized caskets for this. Goddammit!" Both canisters would have to be opened and the remains transferred into bags. Jimmy and Marcus looked at him and said nothing. No one really wanted to see what the condition of the men inside was like, how these oilmen might look after a helicopter crash in India had brought them to the funeral home.

Para ordered the boys into action. "Slim, bring down those sealed caskets, the bronze ones just inside the door to the right. Damn! We've already pulled the lining out of that one. The funeral home will have to cover the cost of using the other kind. Maybe we'll take it out of Jack's salary," he said with a smile. "Dietz can fix that one up again," he said, pointing to the casket that they had originally chosen. Para found a pair of tin snips and a cold chisel and hammer in the toolbox next to the ambulance. He put his work gloves on and began to beat a hole in the top of one of the boxes. An evil-smelling gas escaped. Para clenched his teeth and continued with the shears, soon making an opening about two feet long and a foot wide, then folded the cut piece back like the lid of a sardine can. The stinging smell grew worse, and Para reached into the box with a bare hand, digging into the sawdust that filled it. Touching human flesh, he turned and spat copiously, saliva pouring. "Damned Hindus! They cremate bodies over there. They just poured some formaldehyde or something over the sawdust. They didn't even try to put the pieces in a bag. We'll have to dig them out. Get some sheets."

Marcus got two plastic sheets from the cabinet and spread one out on the garage floor as Para began, drawing forth sawdust and blackened body parts and putrefying limbs and entrails and bones and a recognizable head, shoveling them onto the sheet with cupped hands. Marcus wretched, and again, and the homemade casket was empty. Para didn't wash his hands or use his work gloves. He spat on the garage floor again, and beat a hole into the second carrier without a word. Again, the gas whistled out, the stench even more overwhelming, and Para hammered and sheared, and swiftly, methodically, transferred the shattered oilman and his damp, stinking sawdust onto the second sheet. Para straightened up. "Cover them with SAFE, and close everything up. Make sure those seals are tightened down good. Do something with those", he said, gesturing toward the emptied tin vessels. "Maybe make a Lysol solution and rinse them out. Chunk them on the pickup. Willie can haul them to the dump tomorrow." He walked to the faucet at the corner of the yard, and rinsed his hands and arms up to the elbows. "I'm going to be late for Mass." That was all he said.

Along the deserted streets, Marcus walked with the sweet taste and sensory detachment of a nap, still within himself, at great peace in the beaming sun and silence of this Sunday afternoon world, with no city noises save the sharp cracking from a pool hall where some greasy kid had just sent sixteen balls into a frenzy with a good break. The Texas Star was closed on Sundays, and getting a cup of coffee took him along three blocks of closed storefronts to a café that he liked, because, in another time, in his high school past, the semi-pro baseball players liked it, too, and would hang around where the local girls, rich and poor ones, could see and flash shy smiles toward them and soon be seduced by these broad-shouldered and strong, swarthy Italians. Then the black-bearded House of David players would be there, and the dignity of the profession was raised considerably over that demonstrated by the sun-browned roughnecks and roustabouts on teams from out of town, and the lean men of the House could have a pepper game so entertaining that the citizens of Guadalupe City forgot who always won the real game that followed.

The café was empty, and Marcus stared down and straight ahead at nothing, his face cupped in his hands, his head propped up on elbows on the counter. The events of the long night before, the putrid flesh of the men in the metal boxes, seemed to have faded into another time.

"Are you okay?" He looked into such a beautiful, pure face, he could only blurt out a single word.

"Yeah."

"May I take your order?"

"Just coffee." He watched as she brought it, fell in love, and had to know who she was. "What's your name?"

"Betty." She smiled. He noticed a thin white scar across her chin, then watched her magic figure as she went through the door to the kitchen. She didn't come back. Time passed. Another waitress came in, tying her apron, and refilled his cup.

Marcus couldn't go back to the funeral home just yet with such racing feelings, and he drifted uncertainly toward Dutch Lane and Willie's house. Velveeta came to the door and directed him into the kitchen. Willie's brown face, usually not much more than a weak tea color, had a gray cast that measured another night of heavy beer drinking and a drunken sleep from which he had just risen. Only a little gold shone as he said hello in a husky voice, his heavy-lidded eyes starting to brighten. Marcus proudly contrived a manly point to make. "I've just met a great piece of tail." Why would he use such a vulgar reference to hide his emotions, to keep from betraying how he was suddenly in love with this sylph, a sweet angel of the restaurant, a woman of proud carriage and comeliness that was rare among us? Willie chuckled, and somehow, Marcus knew that the statement was interpreted properly, that Willie had seen past his bravado to the sweetness that a young man feels for a girl.

"Where?"

"At the Corner Café," he answered.

"Did you find out who she was?"

"Only her first name."

"Why didn't you find out her last name and where she lived and whether she was married or something?"

"She left before I could ask her, and I didn't see a wedding ring," Marcus shrugged. As Willie talked, he punched a hole in a can of evaporated milk, twisting the butcher knife to enlarge the hole.

"Carnation milk," he said, pouring generously into his coffee, "is better." "I heard that at the Pet milk plant, people wash their hands in the milk." His shaky hangover was even more obvious as he carefully unwrapped a package of cinnamon rolls, licking the icing from the cellophane. "Want some coffee and a sweet roll?" he asked.

"Thanks, I do," and they proceeded to eat, occasionally sopping the rolls in the coffee.

Marcus thought about the enchanting waitress constantly, called on Monday, and Tuesday, his anxiety now nervous and growing. The annoyed owner of the Corner Café hung up on Wednesday when Marcus asked for Betty's last name, just after he told him that she hadn't shown up for work after the Sunday before.

❧ 11 ❧

Willie and Marcus had a soft drink under a massive pecan tree that was old, perhaps more so than the oldest gravestone. The tent had been erected, and everything was ready to lay that good Christian fellow to rest behind the small white church of weathered boards. The open casket stood in front of the altar, embellished by two racks with a few sprays of store-bought flowers. On the floor in front, by the effort of a poor farmer, proud wildflowers, yellow, red, and pink, of such waving freedom once but now pulled from the land and tamed in a coffee can encircled with aluminum foil, could not go on and fell wilted down its sides.

Lemony sweetness circulated around them from the late-spring gardenias, or maybe it was the magnolia that graced this tolerant little cemetery.

"Have you ever been married, Willie?"

"Once. I reckon we're still married. Never did get divorced. She just left one day and I don't know or give a rat's ass where she is. The day she left, we were arguin', and she hit me right in the eye with a high-heel shoe. The doctor thought I might go blind in that eye, but it healed okay."

"Ever had any kids?"

"Not with her." Willie did not elaborate.

They drank in silence, listening to the pleasant, airy sounds of random bird life in the cemetery.

Gnats found them, crawled into the corners of their eyes, into their ears. They waved them away. "Dog-prick gnats," Marcus said, fanning one-handed. "That's what a friend of mine used to call them. He'd say, 'First on the dog's prick, then on the butter.'"

They fell silent again.

"You came from a big family, Slim?" Willie asked.

"Yeah. Four boys and four girls."

"What did your dad do?"

"Nothing, mostly. He tried being a farmer. Problem was, he was about the laziest person I have ever known. We never had a pot to piss in."

"You must've had a hard time growin' up. Poor folks."

"We weren't even that," Marcus chuckled. "To be poor you had to have something. We had less than poor. We had nothing. We were desperate, or destitute, or something."

Willie just smiled and nodded his head in agreement.

"Indeed we were poor," thought Marcus.

When Marcus' older sisters arrived in Guadalupe City that first summer there, each had bright red eruptions on her hands, long gloves of rash from the disinfectants they had used in their work in a frozen-food-locker plant. All were now moving to another house, where three beds were to be set up for the five males on a porch that would be enclosed with plywood. It was a short trip of about a mile from Parsifal Street. The house, one small bedroom for the three unmarried sisters, a front room for the dining table, and a kitchen, was set on a cramped space niggardly blocked out in a cornfield. Corn grew within a few feet of the porch sleeping area. They would have to wait for another move to have indoor plumbing and running water, but there was a hog pen, and a pen for a *milch* cow, so the possibilities for food were improving. Marcus had never seen so many roaches. The cabinets were alive. The father brought an electric sprayer from the feed store, filled it with fly spray, and began to fog the kitchen. Swarms of roaches appeared on the walls and ceiling, began to stagger drunkenly, and dropped. He hurried outside, puked from breathing the spray, returned, refilled, and kept spraying. Piles of the inverted villains were swept up, but the survivors, although reduced in number, were still running unchecked that night.

Marcus was left at home to care for three little sibs. One day, out toward the paved road that led to town, from the direction of the tar-papered Rendezvous Club, a lone figure walked toward him along the gravel lane that led to the house. An old man, wearing a stained felt hat, frayed and dirty clothes, and a long overcoat on a summer day, came up, looked at Marcus and the three little ones a while, and called him over to the road. It scared him. He asked Marcus for a drink of water. Marcus filled a tin can and took it to him. The man drank and handed back the can, took off his hat, nodded, and politely murmured his thanks. Reaching into his pocket, he took out a Fritos bag, unrolled it, fumbled inside, and produced a nickel. The offer was declined. He smiled, his bristly face lifted, he uncovered his head, said thanks again, and replacing the nickel in the greasy little bag, walked on, as if going nowhere in particular, and was soon no longer visible.

School started. The sixth grade. Marcus had no work now, no money for a Grapette soda, no crackers and summer sausage, no R.C. Colas. His older brother, with his gas-station job, and his sisters, working as waitresses in the bus station, helped a little, and even subsidized, when they could, a lunch for him in the school cafeteria, an order of magnitude improvement over a potted meat sandwich on stale bread. They had a cow penned up now, and every day after school, the littlest brothers cut Johnson grass from along the road and brought it to her. The poor old animal, crippled by a bad hip, never produced milk, and after weeks, was hauled to the auction, to reappear in a can of potted meat or its equivalent. Saturday was payday, and all waited all day for the father's evening arrival in the panel truck with some groceries. He seldom had much pay coming, having borrowed down on it in advance as the days passed. The food never made it through the end of the week, and they were at last reduced to eating onions, the only thing in the house, with mustard.

An ice storm, deeper and colder than any older residents had ever seen, caught them with a thick, punishing cover of sleet and freezing rain. No heat, almost no food, and no options. The father got out somehow and returned with a small space heater and a bottle of propane. This they sat around, fully clothed, and stared at the cracking cold outside, waiting, like Charles Russell's cow, for the Guadalupe City version of a Chinook, a warm southwesterly wind that brings sun and recovery. As the last of the propane burned away, it did become warmer, and they could bask outside, finding hundreds of birds, ambushed by the sudden, unnatural weather, dead in the rose hedges and around the cow pen. And on the local news, Marcus heard that an old man in an overcoat had been found dead, covered with hay in a barn not more than two or three miles away.

Late spring, a move again, back to Parsifal Street, into a bigger house that had a bathtub and toilet, added as an afterthought, almost outside, on a boarded-up screened porch. This house of darkness and tragedy, freed by the tenant just killed when a wall-sized slab of concrete toppled on him at work, became home, where bare light bulbs hung from the high ceiling, their wires crusty with fly excrement. But they now had natural gas piped in, and even a refrigerator, a box with a round compressor on top that hummed aloud and vibrated, but managed to keep things cool, sometimes made ice, and secured food from the quick and resourceful roaches. Chile pequin peppers grew plentifully around the back steps and under a rainwater cistern, and alongside, fig trees that were richly fruited in the hot summer. Toward the back, thick stands of bloodweeds blocked the view of fields of maize and cotton beyond. Again the roaches fouled the kitchen until a bargain-priced pest exterminator made an offer to get them out. He sprayed in and around, and roaches fell from the ceiling and cabinets onto the sheet-metal countertop like the sound of drizzling raindrops.

The roaches stayed. The man returned, and with high-pressure guns, sprayed under the house and around the blocks that held the house about two feet above the ground and out of the inevitable river floods. The roaches were thinned out, but held on. After a third trip, another failure, the man refunded their money and left without apology or excuse. The roaches were merely scattered; one crawled onto the back of the pew from a sister's dress as she sat in church while the other sister watched in embarrassed horror as it ran along the edge behind the backs of their fellow worshipers.

On the shoulder of the highway to The Valley, under the overhang of an abandoned service station, Marcus' wet little school group waited for the bus approaching in the drizzle. In the distance Marcus could see it. He stepped out just as a flatbed tractor-trailer jackknifed and crashed through with a sliding, ugly sound, implanting frozen images of his friend Sonny tumbling head over heels, glasses flying, and Sonny's sister, her head split across and her pouring blood spreading into the rain and gravel. Then Marcus was hit by the trailer. He heard ringing, and then felt nothing. In a while, he was aware that he lay next to the pillar of the service station and could not speak or open his mouth, and the globe of his head ached across its entire circumference. The mother of his friends raced up from her little wooden house on Parsifal Street, apron still tied, and screamed in her shrill high voice, "Sister, Sister, Sonny, Sonny," alternately comforting her moaning daughter where she lay twisted, and stroking the head of her unconscious son, squeezing his crushed, windowless glasses in her palsied hand. And the ambulance came and took them, and Marcus boarded the school bus that waited with its shocked and wide-eyed student witnesses. He tried to make it. By mid-morning, the light from the windows had a strange glow, and he began to shiver and cry and was called to the front of the room with orders to explain. Speaking through closed teeth, he said that "a truck hit me and hurt my head, and I think my friend might die." The teacher requested more details, and again his experience was told, now through flooding tears. *Mama, mama, come down and help me.* At last, he was taken to the office, the father was called, and Marcus was seen by the school's recommended doctor, a man with a cloudy face, liquid eyes, a thin mustache, and a reputation around town for having taken too many self-prescribed narcotics. He examined Marcus' swollen temple and took his blood pressure, and with casual dismissal diagnosed a concussion. There was insurance money, Marcus heard later, either seventy-five or one hundred dollars, put in trust, with the father as custodian. A fortune that large inspired many daydreams. He asked the father about it, and again, "When do I get the money?" Then one day the father roared back, saying, "If I hear one goddamned more word about that money, I am fixing to slap you until the snots fly." His compensation for suffering obviously gone, the bank account empty, the daydreams ended right there.

Mid-summer, and the incinerator at the cotton gin across the highway to and from The Valley began its annual eruption, sending waves of white smoke that smelled of burning cloth blowing through the open houses of poor people on Parsifal Street. Construction closed the highway, and slow-moving tractor-trailer loads of onions and tomatoes and cucumbers and watermelons shook the house through the day and night on their detour north to cross The River and find the citizens in some distant town. Sonny recovered and wore new glasses that didn't have the wraps of adhesive tape he had always needed to hold the old ones together. He told Marcus of his father's dream, as they walked along the trail through the field of blood-weeds behind his house, that Sister as a baby was found broken and dead there, and his father promptly sold the land to keep the dream from coming true. And Sister did continue to young womanhood, only now she had a deep pink scar that angled across her forehead, a facial blaze reminding her of the brutal, skidding truck. They found alligator gars in the narrow gut of the bayou behind Sonny's house, two feet long and longer, swimming slowly back and forth on the surface of the thick, shallow pools, easy targets for the crude arrows that they fired into them from homemade willow bows. They carried the gars, five or six at a time, still slapping and protesting, to the Mexican family of many children, where the fish were welcomed, and in exchange, the grateful mother gave the boys coffee cans filled with dewberries, mostly green, that she called "dew-bears."

Sonny's mother kept their small home on her end of Parsifal Street in spotless order, and Marcus was conscious of her attempts to beautify a place with floorboards so gapped that the ground beneath the house was visible. He saw devotion in the starch-stiffened clothes she ironed for her children, self, and husband, who sweated the shirts into limp wrinkles soon after donning them. On a table in the middle of the main room, bell-like and ruffled, pomegranate blossoms were formed into a bouquet of deep, pure orange more beautiful than any arrangement of orchids ever created. Sonny said that the obnoxious buzz of a single katydid kept at least three houses awake on these sultry nights when no breeze moved and no relief from the heat came with darkness.

Marcus found a job, and was glad to be earning eight dollars a week washing dishes in a simple café that served hamburgers, hot dogs, fried ham sandwiches, and a few other things in the front half of a bakery. The waitress liked him and would sneak food to the back where he worked. It didn't last, and her nimble hands in the cash register, taken together with her habit of placing a cloth over the mouthpiece of the phone when she made her mysterious calls, accelerated her dismissal out the door and away. Marcus was pressed into service by Mrs. Miller as a waiter, and soon discovered the joy of finding a nickel or two in tips on the tables after-wards, even though he refused to smile at the guests because the gap of the missing front tooth so completely embarrassed him. More work was found in the bakery, and Mr. Miller would come in from his daytime sleep with instructions for that night's output. Then Marcus burned his arm on an oven, a three-inch blistered wound from the inside of his wrist halfway to the elbow. It would have been inconsequential, but the constant immersion in dishwater in short order led to a weeping surface of raw, draining, infected flesh, and Mrs. Miller, turning the arm and looking at the hurtful lesion, saying nothing, offering no ointments to lessen its mortification, told him to stay in the back and away from the customers out front. A new dishwashing boy was hired, and Marcus was elevated to a promising occupation as a baker's helper, and his pay was increased, with a sacrifice. Now he would be working nights, alone, ten at night until six in the morning, six days a week—fifteen dollars, less Social Security tax.

He began. He soon discovered the impossibility of sleeping in the daytime in a house where the bed felt like fire and the racket of sibs drifted in and out all day. Nothing seemed to make sense. The father drove him to work and went home to bed. He unlocked the bakery, boiled a hundred pounds of potatoes, skinned them, beat them into the doughnut dough, and started the ovens and the oil in the doughnut fryer. In the night, unreal thoughts were laced together in his mind, and he fought against sleep while the whine of the big exhaust fan overhead flowed in and out of his consciousness, blending into the fractions of sleep until he jerked awake and slid off the flour sacks where he rested. Unnatural sights and sounds repeated themselves, and he heard the music of a Gulf Oil commercial and the themes of TV shows in the singing of the fan, and his cousin's picture of a naked German girl with her legs spread open and her head tilted to her shoulder, and he had never seen a woman's private hair before, and he couldn't stop thinking about what he saw over and over in the white, fluorescent, floating space surrounding him. He drank leftover coffee from the café in front and worked at staying awake, and fried doughnuts, flipping them in the oil with sticks like a practiced drummer, and icing them and dressing them in careful rows on trays until the last was done and it was four o'clock. Mr. Miller came in, loaded, and left for his deliveries to the bus station and yawning night people at the all-night cafés and motels along the Houston highway. He mixed and rolled and cut the cinnamon rolls and left them to rise with the sun as he walked home at six, down Main Street that mostly slept still, and on to The River and across. In the house, last night's dinner dishes and remnants still lay on the dining table, and a long, long time had passed while he fought against sleep and worked in a kind of weirdness, and yet his place at the table and remains of tough roasting ears remained undisturbed where he had eaten the night, the day, the long time, before. He fell into a pitifully shallow, hot sleep, to wake up confused. Was that the evening sun or the morning sun? Did he sleep through the night and miss going to work? It began again, and the father went back to his bed and to sleep, and Marcus opened the bakery, watched in the black sky by the angel of his mother, weeping and weeping for her second boy who dreamed, dreamed of sleep and rest. *Mama, mama, come down and help me! My nose is bleeding, and I must hold a rag to my nose, and I must do my work with one hand until it clots and stops.*

School, the seventh grade, and Marcus went to the bakery at four in the morning to finish frying doughnuts and go on delivery runs and walk to school carrying with himself a cloud of grease and frying smells, and he hears the jokes about that in class, but he can't produce a smile because he is ashamed of a great space where a strong frontal tooth once was. But Mrs. Hacks comes over and puts her hand on his shoulder and tells the class that they should have manners like his and should write as beautifully with the fountain pen as he and that he is the best student in the English class, and he is lifted up for a little while. The nosebleed starts, and he begins to walk home along North Street, and the nosebleed stops quickly, and somewhere he has read that exercise increases the sugar in the blood and makes blood clot more rapidly, and the effulgence of clear, wintry daylight, delightful sunlight and outside air feel so good. He thinks about the slim, balding man who always wore a coat and tie and drove a modern car, sometimes a Cadillac that pulled up to the front door of the bakery, and he wondered about his wealth, until he was told that the bald man was a used-car salesman from the lot next to the Lutheran church, and he drove different cars hoping to keep the batteries up on his collection. The English teacher from high school would come in early with her husband and ask for something "just out of the oven". It was usually cinnamon rolls or a cherry or prune *kolache*, or maybe an apple one. They were nice people who spoke softly and would stop and offer a ride to school, apparently ignoring the greasy emanations of bakery air from Marcus into their closed car.

At last he has saved enough to buy a tooth to fill his smile's gap, and the father will take him to the four-fingered dentist because that dentist made dentures for some old man and "you couldn't tell that they were false teeth." So Marcus is back in the four-fingered dentist's chair. Without a word, the man takes a gauze pad and rubs the yellow scum off the upper front teeth. With no encouragement or explanations, and again, no anesthetic, he begins to grind with a slow, hot electric bit. As nauseating burning bone rises into Marcus' nose and the pain grows, the dentist shoves his hand under the chin and stops his slide downward in the chair, and with an audible sigh of impatience, shoves him brusquely upward, and Marcus can no longer evade the burning bit. He grinds and rinses, grinds and rinses, and with another weary sigh, finishes at last. The impressions are made, and he paints something intensely organic on the newly ground tooth. A week later, Marcus has the new central tooth bridged in to a side fixture where gold shines round the sides of the stem of the tooth that remains as its anchor. Within a couple of weeks the bridge falls out, and it is glued in again, and again, and it falls out and the main tooth breaks in two on the sidewalk. Marcus ties the halves together with thread, and finally there is no money left to get it glued in again, and now the space has a worse-looking ground stump.

It's cold, and there is ice on the windshield of the panel truck when Mr. Miller makes the rounds with the doughnuts, and in the clear and starry cold Marcus thinks that his mama can see him better now, and he can sleep a little better on Saturday after a nightlong shift. Mutti, his German grandmother, comes to visit and tells him that she is proud because he has a good job and will *bei Gelde sein* when he grows up, more so than her coarse and alcoholic half-brother who runs a shrimp boat out of Port Gillette and was also said to "make good money" by the family. With her gray thin hair pulled taut and wound into a doughnut-sized roll atop her head and her wireless glasses, she looks unchanged, but she is older and bent and sad and begins to tell how her son and daughter-in-law and the sixteen children have treated her and how her own son has shouted that she is the first to stuff her *Fresse* with food. Mutti's tears of misery pour down her corrugated face each day until she goes back to her home on the bluff in the pineries to be with her eighteen family persons who have no kindness for her. *Mother of my mother.*

School's out, and summer returns with the ten-to-six shift, and nosebleeds become worse during the night's work and strangle and wake Marcus from a fretful sleep in the simmering daytime. He is so tired. Blanched. Hollow-eyed. Mr. Miller returns from his deliveries, sits, lowers his untanned night-worker's face forward, and talks. In kind and deliberate tones, he tells Marcus that he must not come to work again. He is not being fired. He just doesn't think Marcus is strong enough and well enough to come back and work through another night. A paycheck will be ready later. He reaches out, their soft, white baker's hands shake farewell, and Marcus walks back across The River. In the gentle afternoon of the bakery, Mrs. Miller hands him the wages, alternately biting her lower lip and pursing her mouth. When tears rose and shimmered in her eyes and spilled onto her cheeks, Marcus said goodbye, turned away from the North Main Bakery and Sweet Shop, and walked across The River again that day to the grocery-feed store where he cashed the check and bought a rod and reel that he had held many times and wanted even longer. His new purchase introduced at home, and his job's end told, a clap of rage fell upon him from the father, with an epilogue that went, "If you are not going to work, then you are not going to buy any goddamned fishing rod. Take it back, and I mean now, or I will tear your ass up, boy." A career as a baker was over, and any joy of fishing was emphatically placed on hold.

Marcus hung around the house and watched the waves of white smoke from the cotton gin flowing between the houses on Parsifal Street and onward. Black wasps and yellow jackets swarmed around the few figs that had a chance to fall and rot in the sun, and the smoke moved on and along and around the corner of Parsifal through a pecan grove where a single docile longhorn stood with a motionless egret and the grass was as clean and cropped as a new-mown hayfield. Mud daubers began their work of hunting spiders under and around the house, and their buzzing sounds in the dirt tubes under the roof of the shed brought to mind again the old debate among the brothers: if a mud dauber tries to capture a black widow, who wins? The spider didn't have a chance. The wasp always dragged its flaccid prey away in the end.

A cousin came forward with a remedy for nosebleeds, and conscientiously fashioned the device that would work. He pulled the lead from a .22 cartridge, flattened it, punched a hole in it and tied it to a thin string that Marcus was to wear around his neck. The miracle happened. The nosebleeds stopped abruptly and never returned, and Marcus kept the little pendant hanging there faithfully, even in bed. Only once had he seen such a supernatural outcome, and that was a long time before, when his mother tied a necklace of bullnettle roots around his little sister's neck to treat her teething pain.

Sonny waited on the porch, afraid to enter the house since the time the father shouted at him for walking uninvited into the room where the five men and a cousin slept. He had a job lead and spoke of a man who needed another helper. Sonny and Marcus were to trap minnows in The River for the bait shops around San Antonio.

At six in the morning Mr. Fischbach arrived in his beaten pickup truck and laid down a few strident, prolonged honks because no one expected him so early. He took the two boys about thirty miles upriver, then left the main road to cut through stands of heavy live-oak woods and clearings of rich brown grasses and sage, the gear in the back tumbling and rolling, and followed barbed-wire fence lines to the place he wanted on The River. There, after about five minutes of instruction, he left Marcus, on the bank opposite a willow-covered island, with perforated garbage cans holding simple supplies and food things, little but a loaf of "day-old" bread, stale and tasting of gasoline, potatoes, soft cheese, matches, some lard in a jelly jar, and a frying pan. Marcus was given a tarpaulin to roll into for the night and told that he would be retrieved the next day about sunset. The truck rattled away, and Sonny was dropped somewhere else, and Marcus worked out plans for catching and holding the minnows. He located the best places to anchor the glass jars into which the minnows were funneled for the dried dog food. Inner tubes circled the necks of the garbage cans staked in the stream and held them upright, repositories for the catch. Serene, The River's rhythms gradually took over, with tidal movements of its warm, clear and blue-green water and sweeping motions of its willows, little bass in the shallows and the union of sounds of cicadas and running water and warm wind tracking The River's course, bearing reflective tufts of fluff as the cottonwoods and dandelions gave up their seeds and insects meandered without purpose in the sun. Traps were emptied, little minnows were sized by the holes in the garbage cans and the bigger ones, red horse minnows, didn't escape and went onward to decorate a fisher's hook. Mid-day, and the sun's eduction of musty vegetable smells from The River's body grew stronger, and Marcus made a meal of bread, fried potatoes, and cheese. The sounds flowed on, blending and ebbing, and he dozed off in the shade.

A blue jay's obstreperous call woke him, and he ran the traps in series, wading back and forth and circling the mid-stream island, stopping to void in the water and watch the bubbles float away. The afternoon ran on, longer shadows crossed The River, and the sounds of the day became subdued and sweeter, as if his solitude, already pleasant, needed even gentler and more reassuring music to usher in the evening. Waist-deep, he washed, and fixed again potatoes and cheese and bread before tying the tarp into a rough approximation of a tent, just before the mosquitoes increased to numbers impossible to deal with and the darkness brought lightning bugs from the grass to rise and flash to each of their kind in the trees. Under the cover, distant sounds of cattle lowing reached him, and nightjars diving from the darkening sky overhead to skim over The River and vocalizing with a peculiar slide-whistle decrescendo that locked onto their insect targets, and crickets and katydids and frogs and unknown singers began to add to the choir of this vesperal time. The North Main

Bakery and Sweet Shop came to mind, and he fingered the lead weight hanging from his neck and spoke aloud of his good fortune to be where he was and free to feel the sunshine and get brown or go to sleep, and he remembered how delicious hot, crisp doughnuts were and missed that. Even more so, he missed coffee the next morning and decided that a few improvements in living conditions would be instituted soon.

Mr. Fischbach returned in mid-afternoon and transferred the minnows to a holding tank on the back of the pickup, and eventually got the right connections made from a tangle of wires pulled from underneath the cab, starting an aerator. They loaded the gear, and found Sonny, waiting, then the boys were dropped off on Parsifal Street, given the two dollars they had earned, and Mr. Fischbach left for a round trip to San Antonio that took half the night. The next morning, he told them with a heavy-lidded, gap-toothed grin that they had caught and he had sold "eighty-eight dollars worth of minners in San Antone," and he was pleased with his team of trappers.

The pattern was set, and the summer moved on with the pleasantries that a little income could bring, the coffee that boiled in the morning and the summer sausage that smelled so good frying in the outdoors. Armadillos became companions, and their studious shuffling along the embankment, rooting here and there, gave Marcus chances to quietly grab their tails and hold firm until they realized their arrest, when they would pause, turn and analyze the problem, and with an absurd look of genuine annoyance pull away as Marcus laughed out loud to himself and them.

At times, Mr. Fischbach would offer the boys brief swimming lessons and taught them how to float on their backs, knowledge that reduced considerably their fears that a misstep in The River, alone, would be their last. He pointed out good places to set out lines, and catfish fried in lard added meat to their refection. He talked, in selected personal glimpses, of the war, his missions as a B-29 tail gunner, the fact that he thought he had seen the *Enola Gay* on Tinian, the wild times in Japan during the occupation. On one of those backwater islands, he had watched while medics amputated the leg of a Marine on a table made of boards spanning two oil drums. "You know," he said, "watching them cut that guy's leg off made such a strong impression on me, I found out what his name was and everything before he was shipped stateside. At my unit's tenth reunion last year, they told me that he came straight home, became a doctor and moved to Alaska. I guess he's up there right now taking care of Eskimos or whatever else lives up there." A short-statured, happy Santa Claus spirit on the banks of The River, until his face darkened and he really remembered the battle days and told them that he had been scared shitless in that turret, and he would look down river pensively, pulling at his unmanaged black beard, and he was far away.

Marcus learned much about the Guadalupe, its tides, its life, its taste, its neighbors. There were clouds, though. Mr. Fischbach complained every day that the carbuncle in his ear was getting worse and that the "pills the Doc gave me didn't do a damn bit of good." He worried about his wife, expected to deliver any day, while he was out with his trapping or making the long drive to San Antonio and back in the night.

A slow drizzle began to fall as Marcus finished his supper, so he dragged his gear up over the bank to a field about a quarter mile back where he had seen a tin shed, an old deer blind or abandoned cover for a feeder of some sort. The tin leaked in places, but the shelter was big enough to keep most of him dry, and he listened to the falling rain and drops on the tarp until late into the night. A soft plop on the pillow by his head didn't seem important until he rolled over and was stung on the ear. Without light, he felt for and mashed the source, and lay awake most of the night, throbbing and wondering. At dawn, he saw the scorpion that he had suspected all along, and his swollen ear, as thick as his thumb, was a testament to its mean venom. "A stinging lizard, huh?" was Mr. Fischbach's comment in the truck on the way back to town. It was Friday, and the weekend would give him a chance to recuperate. It didn't matter, though, because Sonny informed Marcus on Sunday that Mr. Fischbach wouldn't be coming again, having given up the minnow business to do something else.

❧ 12 ❧

Para prepared his materials to give Marcus a haircut in the preparation room. Near the wall Para had an oak dresser that he was refinishing, preferring to enjoy his hobby in the room with the best air conditioning. On the embalming table, an elderly gentleman lay dressed and ready for a casket.

"You did a good job there, Frank," Marcus said, looking at the man and then the piece of furniture.

"Well, I do the best I can, trying to make old things look better than they did before."

It was a rare moment of levity in the presence of the dead. With all of the jokes and obscenities thrown around by the fellows in the funeral home, disrespectful comments just weren't tolerated around the bodies nor was irreverence used as procedures ensued during their casketings and burials. Para became especially angry one day and snapped at Marcus and Jimmy after they exchanged a worn remark while Para embalmed a thin, older woman from the convent across the street. "She's a nun. That means she ain't had none and don't want none," Jimmy said. Para got to the point quickly. "Hey, boys, knock it off, and I mean right now. Don't talk that way in front of a Sister." Para's Catholicism and his deep, well-balanced sense of dignity spoke for him.

In the cool white light, Para began by oiling his electric clippers, his cigar lit, adding a human touch to the united smells of varnish and embalming chemicals.

"I've noticed, Slim, that you don't always stand up straight. You always favor your right side, like you're leaning over." Para's observation reflected his fatherly concern for the college students, and he continued as Marcus took a seat on the stool. "Were you born that way?"

"No, this happened about six years ago. I've had a little trouble ever since."

"What happened? You still seem to be able to handle the cots and do the heavy lifting around here all right."

Marcus told him the story of his broken spine.

Word had gone up and down Parsifal and the other Wagnerian streets that a Mr. Garcia was looking for farm labor, and Marcus contacted his son, who told him where to wait for a ride to the maize fields, and he became a flagman for a crop duster. The loud, yellow biplane would roar just overhead, ejecting a cloud of spray that washed over Marcus and the rows of grain as he held a red flag aloft, and the plane would rise, bank, and make the next pass, guided by a new position a few steps over. That field finished, the pilot flew from sight just above the treetops, and Marcus felt for the first time the burn of pesticide soaking his clothes and the ballistic aftereffects of insect killer flailing bare arms and face, and the heat of the sun, and he was taken to another field, and a little while later the pilot came again at treetop level, and Marcus vectored him in, one swath after another. The burning on his skin was worse now, and he hated the feel of the sun on his fiery arms and neck, but the day was over after the fourth field. He washed over and over in cold water, glad to be done.

Two more days of this and Mr. Garcia said that Marcus could pick cotton if he wanted to, and he jumped at it, not really finding any excitement in being a flagman again, or even enjoying the nostalgic feeling of a plane throbbing overhead, and besides, he could walk to the fields and didn't have to depend on making connections for a ride, and he always found conversation awkward in the pickup cab of a driver-boss, anyway. About fifteen people showed up the next morning, picksacks were distributed, and Marcus worked, the only non-Mexican, non-Negro among them, for a "dollar a hundred." Older, wiser pickers wore knee pads cut from old tires and methodically grabbed cotton, two rows at a time with flying hands that pumped into the sacks slung around their necks and dragging along behind.

The sun beat upon their backs, and its vertical heat was made stronger by the practically cloudless sky and windless weather, and they would look up and turn, stretch and crack and straighten, mop away the sweat under the bands of their straw hats, and scan the universe hopefully for a sign that some shade might come from somewhere on the horizon. When enough was picked, they hoisted the picksacks over their shoulders and carried them back to the high trailer and weighed them, announcing the amount to Mr. Garcia, who sat under a tree and penciled in the values in a composition book, in Marcus' case under his misspelled name, critical and watchful as the hands emptied their lots into the trailer, with its familiar scorched smell of cotton, to make sure they weren't grabbing too many bolls and leaves, which produced trashy bales. Under the trees and under the trailer with their lunches, easy attitudes flowed among all the pickers and the Negroes would laugh with each other and talk of the prices of things in the store or their mishap on "June-teenth," when the car broke down as they were going "up the country to Dime Box" and they missed the barbecue. By Saturday noon, when they quit, Marcus had earned almost nine dollars, and never quite matched the output of the others, although he tried in earnest to keep up.

The summer could now be measured, row by shimmering row, dollar by dollar, and by the accumulation of open cuts on his fingers where the sharp spines of the cotton bolls dug in and by the occasional wasp that stung him or tried to when he jostled a nest hidden in the vines that draped the cotton stalks every few yards. He really came to appreciate the expression "being in high cotton" when the merciful obliquity of the sun in the afternoon meant that a little shade was cast on them and on the paths between the rows: the higher the cotton, the more shade on the hot dirt. As the day wound down, the Negroes would hum hymns less frequently and would wearily sigh more assertively, and the rapid language of the Mexicans faded, and fatigue and strain and shoulders chafed where the sack looped across made all the field hands concentrate internally on gathering the last of that day's cotton before Mr. Garcia signaled quitting time.

Trine Contreras was Marcus' best friend out there, and they always did their best to pick side-by-side, telling their stories non-stop. Back in the sixth grade, Trine had given Marcus rides on the back of his bike, and his strength in pumping both of them up the long grade from City Park and The River north to the wealthy part of town was phenomenal. Their teacher repeatedly called him "Tryne" like "brine" with a long "i," and he had no nerve to identify himself as "Trini," but now he was evolving into independence as a real *pachuco* in school with his pants pulled down off his waist and greased hair back in ducktails and steel taps on the heels of loafers that he noisily scraped along the sidewalk with a slouchy shuffle. Trine carried an excessive switchblade that made the average pocketknife look foolish in contests of mumblety-peg in the schoolyard. If he had any malicious intent with his knife, he never mentioned anything, and his knife was always with him, even in the fields. As they moved along, he graphically boasted that a classmate of theirs had been generous with her favors and that he had an oral encounter with her body the week after school ended. His descriptions of his activities in her pleasure area had Marcus distracted, fantasizing and visualizing in his unexposed pubescence what may be offered to him also some day. Trine was unquestionably a man of the world, and Marcus envied his accomplishments. He could also "cotton" with the best of them in the fields, thin, musical fingers moving in perfect concert.

The money that Marcus earned in the fields served him well, and he entered the eighth grade with a new blue jeans and couple of shirts from the city's original J.C. Penney store that still carried bills and receipts over a clever moving network of ropes and pulleys and canisters not much bigger than a baby bottle that raced upstairs, down, and across. He couldn't afford shoes right away; his brother, however, brought from the service station a pair of run-down high-top work shoes that he was able to polish and make look almost presentable, although their oversized length and brass shoestring hooks were obvious as he plodded across the campus. The father spoke to the owner of the grocery-feed store, on the highway to The Valley, about a job, and Marcus began to work after school and on Saturdays for forty cents an hour, a magnificent wage that he knew to be almost fifteen cents more than that paid the sackboys at the Syrian-owned stores just north of The River.

Only Johnny Montez had a comfortable view of the job. Missing the three middle fingers on his right hand, he used the thumb and little finger as dexterously as five, and virtually skated around the store, steel shoe taps clicking, never stopping, always working and moving, the consummate employee. "Johnny," Marcus asked one day as he watched him arrange potatoes with both hands at equal speed, "what happened to your hand?"

"When I was seven years old, my brother was playing with a lawn mower, the kind that has a 'rill' and you push around, and I was lying in the yard, and he played like he was going to run over me, and he shoved it at me, and I threw up my hands, and the fingers were cut off, just like that." Even as he told this, Johnny, this thin wiry boy from a poor family, smiled, and when Marcus imagined the horror of that cruel shearing of an innocent child's fingers a long time ago by a mower reel and sensed Johnny's unexpressed sadness, their working comradeship was cemented.

Little about working in that grocery store was fun, except the occasional cold cuts that Marcus sneaked from the meat counter and ate surreptitiously elsewhere and the apples or bananas or plums that likewise never made it to the customers. Always, the pacing guardian of the store was there in body and spirit, and angry, vehement words from the front warned them not to make mistakes, as had Miss Enderlie, the checker, who stood red-eyed, bawling, and apologizing for having taken a hot check, now waved in front of her wet face, and Cecil's unfortunate error, stupidly giving a customer a paycheck back, accepting the check stub as the real thing. Once in a while, a gentlemanly buyer for a ranch with a well-known name would come in, and the lucky sackboy who carried the hundred-pound sacks of potatoes and the heavy boxes of groceries to his truck would earn an unbelievable tip of as much as a dollar. The boys rushed to be there for these visitors. Most of the time, though, overloaded bags and boxes and wooden lettuce crates filled with canned food required all of their strength to handle, and the irritation that Marcus felt for husky farmers who watched passively, not lending a hand, expecting service from a struggling schoolboy, even Johnny, was exceeded only by the fear that a ripped bag would have glass things falling and breaking in the sight or hearing of an unforgiving boss.

All in all, it was an even-tempered time, and his earnings were suffi-cient to have yet another bridge made for him by the four-fingered den-tist; he had some new clothes, plenty to eat, stolen or otherwise, and hot dogs and ice cream treats that Trine and he would buy across the street from Junior High at a place called Allen's Drive-Inn where the "Houseburger" smelled like spoiled meat.

A preventable calamity stopped Marcus' progress. Christmas approaching meant that fireworks would be sold from stands across The River on the highway to The Valley. Tin cans, upside down, the fuse of a firecracker sticking out of holes in their bottoms and pressed into the mud, could be launched straight up. One didn't go off, and just as Marcus bent over to pull the can up, the presumably dead fuse did its job, and the flying can cut his lower lip completely through, shattered his bridge, and bloodied his nose. Mrs. Sattler, a neighbor, ran to him quickly and placed a wet towel on his mouth and nose. She hurried back to her home, and called the father, who flew up to his house in the red panel truck and then sprint-ed across the yard toward the boy, loosening his huge belt as he ran. He started whipping Marcus violently, reminding him with each stroke that he had been warned not to play with firecrackers, ignoring the blood fusing with tears of shock and pain until Mrs. Sattler threw her portly self between his raised belt and Marcus. His rage was then vented on the pleading Samaritan. "This is none of your goddamned business, and I'll whip my kids when I goddamned well want to." Then he stopped, walked to the panel truck, fastened his belt, and went back to work. Shaking, the good neighbor went home. Marcus walked to work. The boss enjoyed a good laugh, and his swollen, extended lip with an ineffectual Band-Aid and broken teeth gave the boss cause for entertaining the store with loud exclamations of "He's been shot!" With the passage of Christmas-season days, the ulcerated, cankerous lip reminded him each moment of his folly.

Business in the grocery store began to drop off that year as customers were attracted to the multiple Syrian-run stores north of The River, where aggressive pricing and a presumed collaboration had wholesalers giving breaks on big lots that Marcus' boss could not afford. Ranchers and farmers who had once come from distances as far as twenty-five miles now abandoned the store, and when school was out for the summer, Marcus got the message that the well-moneyed boss would not pay forty cents an hour to a poor adolescent who needed to earn his food. A cousin took Marcus to the father's brother, married to the mother's half-sister, a union that produced cousins of a kinship that was stronger than usual. Out of the city limits, they punched the opener through the first two cans of two six-packs of Falstaff and let the icy beer spew its deliciously fungal taste and smell over them, and each lit a King Edward cigar, and Marcus could sense the cool, almost chilling alcohol flowing in the circulation of his arms and trunk. Hot wind funneled into the car through the cocked vent windows of the '50 Ford, and his floating, heady perceptions, his powerful, manly self-assessment at that time made the highway, straight and flat, a river underneath of moving concrete and stone and unstoppable destiny.

At the end, relaxed and happy, he did not know that their slow descent along the winding road of the green bluff to the Colorado was taking Marcus to a near experience with death, his first.

His aunt greeted him warmly in her high, unpleasant voice and speech that let each word linger a while as a little girl in song, and his uncle shook hands vigorously, the metronomic twitching of the right side of his face, coincident with air sucking through his eyeteeth-premolars, gave his words a clucking "*tsk-tsk*" punctuation. In their tin-roofed farmhouse, with the four children living there, and at their table, Marcus was welcome. His aunt gave him a bright yellow shirt of pure, impenetrable nylon—"crinkle crepe." Hot, smelling of strong sweat when he wore it, he went to the Meat Club on Saturdays, where a tough steer was cut up and distributed to the members, and turned the grinder for that night's chili. His aunt always surmised as she served the roast for Sunday dinner that the least tender of animals were donated by her neighbors, but she vowed to sacrifice only a well-fed young calf when it was their family's turn to slaughter for the Club because it was a Christian thing to do.

The cotton was open now, white puffs imbedded in green, small, rounded lobes within a landscape that, were it cerulean, would have vaguely mirrored the towering, pure cumulus cloudscape above. Below the pineries, the creek had given up a few bass and catfish, and along the banks they killed perching doves with a .22, and the summer heat had built to its limit as they settled into their routines in the fields, challenging each other to pick more, to have more weight to raise the levered arm of the cotton scales when they brought the picksacks in. Again, " a dollar a hundred" for the two cousins and a few neighbors who came to help out. With an R.C. Cola from the store next to the gin, they hung on the sides of the trailer as sweaty men covered with lint and dirt vacuumed the cotton out and heard their loud cursing when an occasional croker sack or something foreign and hard flew into the saws and caused the roaring operation to stop for repairs and untangling. The farmers drank beer in small groups and talked of cotton prices, bales to the acre, boll weevils, and a troubling forecast for rain that nobody wanted right now. Money was coming in, and the mood of these affable, sunburned men was pleasant and rich with good-natured jokes about a bull that had "broken his pecker" when he dropped off the cow and was now useless for servicing anything.

Marcus' cousin, exactly his age, was too young to drive a big John Deere, but the boys were feeling grownup and proud because they had pulled the engine apart and reassembled it perfectly when they found water in both cylinders and decided to repair it. Marcus' only worry related to the flywheel that he spun to get the popping engine started, having heard that it could kick back and break an arm, and there was a strange story that a drunk and boastful boy in Fayette County had tried to stall a John Deere engine by squeezing the power takeoff with a croker sack, only to have his arm get caught in the sack, twisted almost off at the shoulder and amputated later. Marcus climbed aboard, standing on the starboard axle next to the seat, hanging on the lever that raised the plows. To his right and almost touching, the tire—as high as his waist as he balanced there, as tall as he when he was on the ground—moved past like a conveyor belt with unlimited power. The cousin accelerated, crossing the open space below the shed, when he, in an instant of inexplicable, thoughtless bravura, locked the brakes on the left rear, steered left, and caused the tractor to pivot in a circle. Marcus was flung outward, the lugs of the tire caught him, stripping the skin from his back, then the lever gave way, and he went down, bent forward, landing on his seat, the wheel of the tractor, now stopped, crushing his face into the ground. He couldn't breathe. Sounds went away. He could hear the loud sound of his heart. He tried to turn over, but his face was pressed to the ground, his mouth open. Still he couldn't breathe. Now, he knew that his life was over, a dark peace. *Mama, Mama, come down and help me.* Then, what began as a hiccup-like twitch in his abdomen became a struggle, a gasp, a little more, another gasp, his mouth in the dirt, and another sharp hiccup, and a quick, shallow bit of air came into his deflated chest. And another.

The cousin began to lift Marcus at the waist and drop him. Marcus rose to his hands and knees, panting, mouth open, and felt some of the rapid breaths coming in, none going out. Long minutes had passed, and he could finally take a breath and exhale in a shaky rhythm. Doubled over, bending to the left, he stumbled to the house.

The aunt made a sad, sympathetic sound when she saw him, the friction-burned skin hanging in translucent pink flaps from his back, the raw exposed flesh, the irregular breaths that sounded like purposeful, deliberate coughs. She rubbed a stinging lotion on his abrasions. Marcus lay on his bed. The sky darkened, and a thunderstorm began with large sporadic raindrops on the tin roof and wind racing through the house. Outside, he could hear men calling and machinery moving to get the trailers under shelter before the rain hit the cotton.

It's night when he wakes, and the family has eaten. His aunt brings him a plate, and the iced tea is so refreshing as he forces himself upright to sit in the darkened room, alone, to eat and fall profoundly asleep again. Voices and loud shouting and the door slams. The room is filled with a strange, orange light, and another shout, "The shed is on fire. The house might catch." Marcus thinks that he must get out of bed; he must get away.

The light is strong and red from the front of the house, and he can see everyone in the yard in silhouette against thundering flames that rise from the ground up as he gasps, grunts to the front porch and props himself against the wall. Embers are falling from the volcanic fountain that was once the barn, and there is so much heat, but mercifully, the wet ground and wet wood from the afternoon shower and the tin roof prevent the sparks' growth into further conflagration. The family talks quietly or not at all. The aunt, searching for any reason to assuage her loss, thinks the fire was set by someone with a grudge and mentions the name that sounds like "Cha'-cha-la". The uncle makes a more levelheaded guess that one of the men had a cigarette in his mouth when he rushed to strip his picksack off in the gathering thunderstorm. In the silence, with the first hints of dawn coming, the noisy, raspy scratching of a cousin's mosquito-bitten legs draws an angry rebuke from her brother.

Three days later, Marcus was taken to town, to see the town's only doctor. He took off his shirt, and took a deep breath, as instructed. The doctor stood behind, but did not probe or feel or ask Marcus to straighten his leaning back. "You have a bruised back," he said. No X-rays, no medicine. Marcus sagged. Surely the pain he was experiencing deserved a more detailed analysis than that. Had the uncle whispered something to the doctor? Was he considered an indolent malingerer? Was the uncle trying to keep the costs of the visit down, thinking of money gone in the holocaust three nights before? *Mama, mama, come down and help me.* The uncle summed up. "If you had broken ribs, *tsk,* you would not have been able to take a deep breath, *tsk.*" The next weekend, the cousin drove Marcus back to Guadalupe City, across The River, to Parsifal Street. Mrs. Sattler came over when she saw the tilted walk, the awkward posture, and asked with a troubled look, "What's wrong with Marcus?" The father sat in a lawn chair on the front porch, his shirt open, his sweaty belly protruding. Without looking at her, he answered, "He's walking lopsided," lit another Camel, scratched around his scrotum, broke wind, and went back to reading the paper.

⌒13⌒

Para had placed his ashtray with its dead cigar on the forehead of the man whose hands now occupied the embalmer's attention, creating an unintentionally comic scene from the deep tragedy of such an early death. The man, hardly more than a teenager, had fallen from a radio tower while painting it, and now Para worked with turpentine to get the brilliant orange paint off the man's hands and from under his fingernails. "This turpentine isn't cutting it, but that's about all I can find around here. If I can just get enough of it off, and pull his cuffs down, and fold his fingers under just right, I might get by."

"It's a shame when young people like this die. What a waste; he's my age," Marcus said.

"Yes, it is, but you talk to some really old people, and they tell you that living a long time might not be that great, either. Your parents are dead, probably some brothers and sisters, maybe even a kid of yours. Anybody who was important to you probably gone. Too much time on your hands, worrying about when you had your last bowel movement, I expect. Worse yet, after a lifetime of trying to do right, you end up in a crappy hole like Rosewood."

Rosewood. What an unfortunate appellation. No roses, just wood. Marcus had been there many times. Some enterprising people had strung together, end to end, a half dozen wooden barracks left over from the war, created a straight hundred-yard, maybe hundred-and-ten-yard corridor down the middle, and placed beds head to toe in the open rooms on either side. "How true," Marcus added. "No privacy whatsoever. We went through there once, and this elderly lady was as naked as a jaybird, having her diaper changed in front of everybody." Mostly, it was the overwhelming smell of urine combined with baby powder that Marcus reacted to, and the fact that at three or four in the morning, when life ebbs, they would have to take a body out, rolling past each bed in sequence from one end to the other on the way in and on the way out. The old people would rise up as the creaks and noises of activity disturbed them, and seeing the cot pass by in the night light with its maroon or blue-black cover, the name McCullough-Shepherd embroidered on the side, they knew that yet another wouldn't be back.

Marcus sat sideways in the big stuffed chair in the office, his legs looped over the arm, watching the wind move the trembling palm fronds and nudge the zinnias that Frank nurtured in front of the sign on the lawn. Swaggering boat-tailed grackles crossed the lawn on foot, emitting that loud hissing call, more like a throttled expiratory screech. "Jackdaws," Marcus thought, "make the damnedest sound." Random pedestrians walked past on the sidewalk out front. The chill of the air conditioning and the overcast outside gave him the sensation of winter that warm day. He thought about his mother. *Mama, I know you are up there.* She really was too young to die, too. Barely thirty-five, all of her teeth gone, giving birth to her ninth child. Eight little ones to raise. The hard work she faced every day. He remembered Gonzales. Her funeral. The hard work.

The Farm in Gonzales had an old Farmall tractor now that the war was over, and the mules, emancipated, wandered around, retired nuisances that broke down gates and entered the hegari fields to trample and graze.

Not even with a bolus of pellets in the ass from that single-shot 12-gauge at long range could the cursing, running father keep the mules from carrying out these raids on forbidden territory. Those mules, linked with reins and leather, sweat and harnesses to the father for so many years, no longer enjoyed any of the respect they once nobly earned as co-workers and field hands.

The red tractor crisscrossed the fields with a disc harrow and created hills for watermelons and sweet potatoes, straining to lay the ground open with a deep-running sweep. Again the old tractor complained and pulled a trailer load of manure from the chicken houses, that same acrid chicken waste so laboriously shoveled out of the windows by all. School ended. The watermelons grew, and crows paid visits laced with malice, pecking each melon just enough to cause it to sour, or rabbits scored them lightly with their teeth, a small insult that nevertheless rendered the melons worthless for the market. Warm days grew hot, and Marcus sat in the fields with a .22, waiting for crows that never came.

Then came the day to load the first truck, and the Florida Giants would be traveling soon. Walter Brown and Pete Gray came and sat in the yard with the father, the three talking quietly. The mother gave them coffee with milk and sugar and to each a treasured orange. Marcus watched the Negroes in shy fascination, studying their contrasting parts in the execution of the task of eating the oranges: the wide mouths, the tongues that seemed so pink against their faces, the white palms of those coarse hands, and the musical movements of their long fingers as they peeled the oranges and stuffed three or four sections at a time into their mouths, noiselessly spitting the seeds as they worked the fruit around.

The morning glories climbed up the posts of the south porch and reached the roof, and mockingbirds always voiced their complicated repertoires through the warm moonstruck nights. Through the generosity of woodpeckers before them, bluebirds came to nest in the fence posts around the barn and in the yard, in a pock-marked pole that brought a single wire to the crank telephone that occasionally worked to link them to others on the party line and beyond. Katydids and crickets added their songs to the night, and grasshoppers grew larger and smarter, evading even the most earnest efforts to slam them to the ground. Having been caught, they ended up in a mayonnaise jar, and with a break from the fields and chicken houses, the boys launched them on willow-pole fishing lines into the scummy earthen tank, just below the house, where the muddy water begrudgingly gave up a small catfish once in a while, yet nurtured a choir of bullfrogs and some sinister cottonmouths.

Midsummer storms roared by with violent thunder. Some deep Lutheran convictions had the parents fearful of punishment from Above at such a time. The rain poured off the roof and cut furrows through the bare dirt that was the yard, driving Dick, mean-tempered hybrid of a bulldog, onto the porch. A rich earth smell filled the air and mixed with the wet smells of the burlap croker sack that was nailed over a broken window. Hail, the most dreadful of calamities to the planter, fell more than once, and covered the yard with a layer of white glistening stones as big as pullet eggs.

Scoured by rain, the ground out near the main road raised pea-sized gravel that was just right for slingshots. Fashioned with strips from wartime red-rubber inner tubes and stocks sawed from pine boards and a projectile pouch made from a shoe tongue, these and a pocket full of little round rocks were a source of much fun and sport. The boys fired away at everything that moved. Only rarely would a hapless field lark, songbird, or quail get caught by their wild shots. Nevertheless, they were proud and remorseless when the flyers fell.

The arrival of the truck from the feed store was cause for true rejoicing among the three older sisters. The oldest and fastest was the first to meet the truck, loaded with broiler mash in cotton-print sacks. They circled the truck, planning their wardrobes, counting the matching sacks, and talking with excited exclamations about the dress or apron that would be created from these hundred-pound sacks with the tiny pink flowers, dull plaids, and childish animal characters printed on them. The mother joined in. The possibilities expanded in her eyes, and quilts and bonnets and shirts for the boys would develop from the sacks piled on the truck. Marcus watched the Mexicans, two of them, unload into the barn, into a special, screened area that kept the ever-watchful rats out. The men began to scuffle, and pushed and shoved each other, first in fun, then in anger, all the while exchanging insults in Spanish. The whole unsettling spectacle finally ran its course, and the empty truck lumbered back to Gonzales.

A hog could be butchered now, but the meat had to be fried, placed in crocks, and covered with thin, runny lard that never hardened. This rancid-smelling "fried-down" meat was later resurrected for meals, with much worry from the mother, who always feared that she would dredge up a rat from the crock near the end. She knew that too many times, when it had cooled down enough to stiffen the fat cover, the rats' bites and footprints were etched in the lard. Gallon jugs of sweet dewberry wine always stood nearby the meat crocks under the kitchen counter, and little glasses of it, like a sacrament of the altar, were given to the sibs because it was "good for the blood."

White summer heat continued, and cracks in the ground grew wide enough to snap a cow's leg. The gray undersides of cumulus clouds fooled them into the promise of relief, but the rare clap of thunder in the afternoon or flash of lightning in the night never brought more than a brief spattering on the dust, if anything at all. Cicadas filled the day with sound, and in the yard the red ants, *die rote Ameisen,* stayed in their hills and off the trails during the middle of the day. The wind was salvation. It always blew. Under the shade trees, though hot, the wind cooled the wet canvas bag, with a red eagle printed on it, that took sweet well-water to the fields and flavored it with a cotton taste. They let it run down their dirt-lined necks as they drank under blessed oaks and watched with curiosity as the father's Adam's apple oscillated up and down his rufous throat with each swallow.

With their bare feet, they hurried and shuffled in the sunshine. In the fields, the tractor pulled a middle "buster" that went deep and rolled the soil over in waves, revealing the peanuts to be separated from the dirt, a grueling process of picking up the plants, shaking the sand free, and throwing them into rows. Grass burrs were woven in with the peanut plants and pricked them throughout the day as they worked in the hot sun. They stepped on them, and pulled them painfully from the horny soles of their feet. Without a sound the mother, too, followed the uprooted rows cut by the old Farmall, her bonnet tied under her chin, bent at the shaking every day with her children, only rarely rising to look up at the shimmering images of the tree line, her hand held to her mouth. A side-delivery rake arranged the peanuts into windrows to be picked up with pitchforks and moved to a thresher that operated in the field. The tractor powered the thresher with a ragged flywheel-and-belt connection that once flew apart, delivering a shocking slap to the side of Marcus's head as he pitched the peanuts into the jaws of the machine. Caked with masks of dust cemented with sweat, the brother and Marcus walked home with the dropping sun these days. Each described how the dollar he was promised would be spent. But there was no dollar, and the reward dwindled to a quarter with the father's summary decision that the peanuts were not in sufficiently high demand to justify the full award of their compensation.

Disappointment seemed to be the father's most persistent offering to his brood of children. He was not accepted, loved, or even present in the minds of his very own brothers and sisters. Aunts or uncles never visited and were seldom mentioned in conversation. When Marcus did see them, they looked different, with the stern, angular faces and thin-lipped looks that reflected their strong German lines and taciturn natures, and they didn't sound the same with their deeply accented words, lapsing in and out of both languages. The father had a round, always-weathered face and was a loud man, who habitually cupped his hand to his ear and strained to hear from the one ear that worked, the other having been deafened when he fell from a cart as a boy and the ear was crushed under its wheel. His teeth never saw a brush, and he chose to rub the surfaces of the few remaining with a wet cloth and baking soda. He seldom bathed or wore clean clothes, pinched his nose, blew the snot on the ground, and wiped his hand on his overalls where he stored Bull Durham and a Prince Albert can that held his cache of kitchen matches. He was big, taller than his generation, and the profuse sweat that he produced usually didn't take long to strip some of the red paint that decorated the Prince.

From the peanut fields to fields of pinto beans Marcus moved in seamless obligation, and he rode the combine to a new set of experiences. Orange-winged and big yellow grasshoppers were swept into the revolving paddles with indiscriminate voracity, and parts of the insects poured into the bags as he diverted the beans from one chute and started the other. Sacks of beans accumulated on the platform, and the tractor stopped for their unloading. He continued, and the dust and fibers had him coughing and expectorating sickly brown phlegm. His sister brought lunch to him and the stranger who towed the combine, and she proudly complemented the buttered sandwiches with a chocolate cake that she had made with lard and bacon grease, giving a flavor to the cake that was disappointingly porcine.

The Baptist preacher, owner of the land on which they lived and paid with the major share of the crops and chickens, would drive up in an old black Ford that had a curious V8 symbol on its beautiful, shiny grill. The preacher would be given a bunch of turnips and beets, roasting ears and chickens, and he would look over the cattle with the JA brand. His car's starter locked up, and they would rock the car to break the starter free. "Preacher Atkinson cussed when his car wouldn't start," Marcus said. The father dismissed him. Then the reverend, in his dark pinstripe suit with a vest, wireless glasses, and hat with a bent brim, gave credibility to Marcus's eavesdropping by declaring to the father, "I'd quit preaching, but goddammit, I need the money!" The preacher stayed for dinner and said grace. The mother had a thin green-pea soup for their meal that day, and it had burned on her primitive stove. The preacher's magnanimity was never as great as when he said at that meager table, "I like it scorched."

The drought held on, and people spoke in their vernacular of "The Droughth," pronounced with a terminal "th." Men arrived and lit long tubes that they had filled with coal oil and pressurized with a hand pump.

These roaring pear burners would rescue the cattle, who now ate prickly pears with the needles singed off, or not, when hunger drove them to eat the cacti with thorns, leaving the tongues of these poor animals so filled with thorns that they couldn't be kept when the cow was slaughtered. All the fields and pastures were fawn-colored and bare, and down near the watermelon patch, the tank shrank into a thick, muddy bowl that forced about twenty or so small catfish to the surface. These were caught by hand and proudly presented to the mother, who rolled them in flour for frying with an expression of disappointment because she didn't have any cornmeal. Under the house they played with doodle bugs in the fine sand, constantly aware of the black widows over their heads, and remembering that when their sister was bitten on the stomach, the doctor made a paste of molasses and baking soda and applied it to the bite on this very sick girl. Rattlesnake bites and pneumonia, like that particular black widow bite, were always spoken of in whispers, being too dreadful to be announced out loud.

The clear-channel station from San Antonio loved them, and gave them news of canners and cutters, cotton and corn and hog prices. The unseen voice told of Mr. Truman's decisions in a Congress as far away as the moon seemed to be, and the family listened during the hot evenings before they washed their feet in a wash tub and went to bed. That radio had brought the crackling static of the round-by-round efforts of Billy Conn until Joe Louis knocked him out, and Tex Ritter singing of a boll-weevil looking for a home, Tommy Dorsey's boogie-woogie, and inspired the children's laughter when grownups reacted to jokes that the young ones couldn't understand. Mostly, though, they were drawn by the pinging theme of radio waves that signaled the noon newscast and the chimes of NBC. This musical train filled the rooms of their open house and carried across the yard to the outhouse, where disturbed iridescent blowflies rose in slow clouds from a foul bed of writhing maggots below and black widows were always believed to be nesting just under the hole.

The mother built a fire around the wash pot and shaved a bar of creamy homemade lye soap into the boiling water. She dipped and prodded the clothes with an ax handle that was bleached clean and white, and lifted them out, steaming, to a Number 3 washtub. Soon a benevolent wind would be whipping and snapping clothes and sheets on the line, producing a friendly sound and giving these ragged belongings a sweetness that they would revisit each time they wore these things or slept on them. The mother uttered a mournful sound and presented to the father a thumb with a splinter driven under the nail for most of its length. He proceeded to cut and pull, extracting the wood with his pocketknife. "I need a new washboard," the mother said, and silently went back to her scrubbing.

Then, when it seemed that the earth couldn't burn more, the wind changed with a gentle sound that passed through the dry, waving fields, then with hard gusts from the south, then from the north. The sky blackened in that direction, and the air now had a cool, delightful feel and an oily smell. "I smell Caldwell," they shouted, and added an obscene vulvar reference, as if that little town of oil fields and watermelons had a female form that produced the odor. The following rain ripped through the countryside and refreshed it with a crystal wash, and sun came out behind it, bright and brilliant, drawing the family to the south porch where the parents sat, drinking strong coffee in the most pleasant of universes.

A year passed. Marcus was now in his eighth year, and it was almost summertime. The mother, gravid with her ninth at age thirty-five, again put her strength into the labor of the fields. Her frame too small for such effort; all of her teeth now gone and her nourishment poor, she handled a plow, guiding it behind the old Farmall as it unearthed Irish potatoes, before leaving one Saturday morning in June to give birth. The little girl lived until early afternoon, and about five hours later, as Marcus' oldest sister sat near her, the mother rose up, said, "I can't hear", and left her children and weeping husband forever.

Then she lay in her casket, dressed in a white shroud prettier than anything she had owned in life, and rested with her baby beside her on the pillow. Sorrow draped the family, even descending on the fields. Watermelons rotted yellow in the sun for miles because there was no market for them then. Fire broke out at the hay baler, and all that was there and everything attached to it burned in a roaring conflagration, while Walter Brown and Pete Gray, who had come shouting, fists hammering on their pickup's doors, beat themselves in frustration, saying again and again, "Lord, have mercy." Chicken prices didn't cover the cost of their feed, and nobody wanted them anyway. Nobody wanted to buy anything. Something was terribly wrong now. Nobody knew what it was, only that something was terribly wrong. Dick died, ill-tempered, snapping half-bulldog that he was, but so steadfastly loyal that he never let a cow near the kids in the yard. Eventually, the screwworm infestations he would get in his back from recklessly tearing through barbed wire fences wore him down, and he curled up and passed away, facing the gate of the front yard where his bovine adversaries had so frequently challenged him. And in the Gonzales paper, where he had read of the "last rites for Mrs. Reel," Marcus saw that others had "rites," and he was confused because they were getting married, and the word didn't make sense. Could their "rites" be the same as those expressed by the piercing wails of his sisters?

⌐14⌐

A truck came to take them from The Farm, and strangers helped load
the family's ragged belongings, even the old living room couch with its
historical rats' nests, for a trip to another town, where Marcus' grieving
aunt, missing her sister, lived. They loaded into the 1934 Chevrolet with
the rusted floor, and left that time and space, still mindful of their mother lying in a place that had been covered by fragrant Indian blankets and
bluebonnets before her grave opened a hole among them.

So they arrived at a new home, but it wasn't an epiphany. The old house
was set in cornfields, and whoever lived there also had to take care of the
dairy herd. The father got that job, having grown up in the county and having known the owner of the land, a benevolent doctor who, unfortunately,
died soon after the family moved in. The management of the dairy and the
supervision of its tenants' activities were then laid in the combined hands
of the owner's widow and an overweight, unemployed son who spent
much of his time flying a maroon and white Stinson that he kept in a shed
at the end of a grassy runway just beyond the yard. And in that house with
walls that creaked with the gusty south wind, the boys were joined by mice
coming in from outside, and in the morning, they found that nightly visitors had brazenly chewed the dead skin off their toes, to the point that after
several such instances, their big toes were pink and raw.

With the winter, snow fell, and the temperature dropped to the lowest ever known, the older people said. It took only a few seconds for the bacon grease poured on the molasses to turn into a solid, hard sheet that shattered as they ate. Scattered through the woods, the dairy cows had a tough time, and lay down to die, while out in the snow, Butch, the white dog, looked oddly yellow.

To the north of the house, in the direction of the sheer green bluffs that rose above a river in the distance, a curious new development took place. Arising from the plain, like a giant tombstone, a drive-in theater came into being. One night, the miracle itself began, and the neon lights shaped like colored stars that flashed on and off, and the name, "SKY HI," in big letters, came on. It was Christmas in the spring, and the great, towering tombstone was its messenger. Big loudspeakers on top broadcast the movie's sound to the patrons, and to the pastures, the cows, and the family. With each changing feature, they were there, sitting alongside the barbed-wire fence that separated the cars from the pasture, and watched, even an unusual public-service movie that featured male genitalia and the scourge of chancroid lesions, about which Marcus knew little. The older brother seemed to have some insight into this, since he sold Cokes from car to car, and often found couples in one state or another during his rounds, which, unfortunately for the couples, began before the movie stopped and the floodlights above the concession stand and over the tower lit up for intermission. The brother's explanations and data about this disease were incomplete, though, and even more confusing were the flaccid, pale balloons that Marcus found in the theater driveway at the highway where he waited for the school bus.

A tooth, last of his baby molars, was pulled by the dentist. The bleeding continued through the night, soaked into the pillow, and left Marcus dizzy and weak in the morning. The dentist packed the socket and pronounced him a "free-bleeder." That he already knew: the merest tap on the nose would send the blood coursing from both nostrils and down his throat. He would sit quietly for what seemed like hours with a rag pressed against his nose, removing it gently from time to time, only to find the hemorrhage restarted. Eventually the clots would fill his nose, where they remained until he eased them out like fat, engorged worms.

One day, the oldest sister let them know that she had quickly married a salesman whom she had met briefly before. The first brother-in-law was an itinerant photographer with an uncertain livelihood and the most interesting face, which featured an asymmetrical mouth; crooked, tobacco-stained teeth; and a few scattered scars on the bridge of the nose and above the eyebrows. He left the sister in the tourist court, came to the house to meet the father, walked up to a short man out by the turkey house, and asked "Mr. Reel?" The man looked at him quizzically, and gestured toward another man working close by. There, as the brother-in-law told it, stood the "biggest goddamned man I have ever seen in my life." So Eddie came into the family, and a few days later, brought his bride, too. He set up his gear, took photographs, and began to merge into the family in a friendly, unrestrained way that complemented his choice of occupation.

Mutti, grandmother, took the seven into her crowded house for a while. In this tin-roofed old place, never painted, set on a bluff under a forest of singing pine trees, Mutti provided for the brother of Marcus' mother and a family that would one day total sixteen children, borne in regular intervals by a wiry suntanned aunt. There were cousins perfectly matched in ages with the Reels, and in an odd way, it became a time for fun and leisure. Food was scarce, and each day Marcus would look at the few eggs that were gathered and saved but couldn't be eaten because they had to be sold. Some eggs Mutti sacrificed to make *kuchen,* getting the wood for the cook stove herself, and finishing her masterpiece by buttering the top with a dried goose wing. At night, she moved around with a feeble kerosene lamp, alternately exhorting or scolding one grandchild or another, rarely using an English word. The uncle, meanwhile, with all his brood, remained an amusing, carefree man. Prone to drinking too much beer at the local grocery store/cotton-gin/gas-station/beer-joint establishment, the uncle's pugilism usually left him the loser. Two black eyes later, he explained that one of the combatants, swinging at him, hit "the fucking gas pump" instead. The word had never been used before in their presence. Uncle delighted in packing as many kids into his 1946 Chevy as would fit, and speeding along the gravel roads to and fro, finding some fictitious cause to slam on the brakes, sending cousins piling into each other and over the seat back, then accelerating again to send them in the other direction.

The steep slopes and thick carpet of needles in the pineries, as they were known, made for fine sledding on barrel staves or pleasant, nonspecific excursions. Near the house, the detritus of living, thrown "over the hill," created a most unseemly mess. Trash and human waste from the bottomless outhouse perched on the hill's edge cascaded down. Further away, the forest was a wonderful, cushioned playground.

Like the passive horned lizards that they caught and led on a leash tied around the horns, Marcus and his brother chopped corn in a perfunctory rhythm, cleaning out weeds, row after row, between the highway and the runway, where that maroon and white Stinson bounced in one day with cotton stalks wrapped around its landing gear after the engine had died and the landlord/pilot had to put it down in some farmer's cotton patch. Their cumulative wages were put into a cheap used bicycle the father bought, the price calculated so as to have money left for himself, but the frame was bent and it broke the chain every few trips, and one day the fork holding the front wheel collapsed and folded under, and that was that.

The father's adventures were too much for the landlady and her torpid son to bear. He had discovered that the woman living in a small decrepit house about a mile below the dairy barn was available and eager, apparently. The young woman, ill bred and stupid, had four children, including an infant, all sired by men unknown. The boys were told to go see her, and Marcus examined her wretched, poor urchins, two older girls about his age, a little boy who squinted sideways with one cloudy eye, and a baby, naked except for a urine-stained diaper. Then the father took her away in the pickup truck and married her. Marcus' aunt, doing her best for her dead sister's children while caring for four of her own on their small tenant farm, was horrified and hurt, but accepted the insult to her sister's memory with resolute dignity. She cried softly as she lowered a milk can into the well where it cooled, and noticing the inquisitive looks of the little sister and brother who lived with her, said in German that she was sorry and did not understand why the father did it. He was promptly fired.

The father found work in a feed store in Guadalupe City. The feed-store manager sent the cigar smoker, John, to move the family in one of their bigger trucks, and ultimately make possible the life Marcus had found in the funeral home.

⤜15⤛

William Shulze, toddler, awoke unnoticed from a nap and left his pallet under the pecan trees of Riverside Park, and in the briefest of epochs within a short lifetime, fell or crawled down the steep bank into The River, and that same soft, melodious ripple of aquamarine water, home to minnows and separator of social status, now showed scant forgiveness for a two-year-old's mistake and took him under and away. Days later, after hints of domestic rifts and accusations of negligence were picked up by the newspaper as the parents apparently laid blame on each other, after dragging and scouring, the boy's gaseous body was discovered floating in the foamy water below the outlet for the city sanitation plant's effluent.

With waterlogged seepage constant from this swollen child, the embalmer's job was made even more difficult by the ragged nips taken from his nose and ears by local turtles and by the crabs that commuted up from Matagorda Bay. Para and Hank worked long into the evening, painstakingly applying and reapplying the colors that would make their adopted son presentable to the public. They continued their efforts in the church on the steaming afternoon of the funeral, adding the black veil draped over his small white casket, but they could give only incomplete, but nevertheless measurable, comfort and reassurances to the mourners, who were so deeply affected by the death of one so young. With ominous signs of a thunderstorm building, the procession went to the cemetery, little William on the back seat of the sedan, Para and the minister up front, McCullough and Marcus following in a second car with seven silent and reflective family members, arriving with the last glint of sun through the faraway silver edges of the clouds and a growing, somber moodiness in the atmosphere. The service began, almost reluctantly, in seeming hesitation, as if to spare all present more grief, more sorrow to be opened afresh by the last of the last rites. The lengthy messages continued in a cadence that seemed slower to Marcus than usual, perhaps because of his perceptions of the exigencies imposed by the threatening weather that moved over and enveloped the cemetery like the closing of day.

By now the sky had become darker than ever, the heavy black clouds took on a greenish tinge, and the light's diffusion evoked fluorescent shimmers that made more beautiful the flowers and the colored fabrics of the bereaved. Unbelievably deep and loud thunder vibrated and shook the thick air, yet not a leaf stirred, not a bit of wind moved the hordes of aggravating mosquitoes that rose from the damp grass where the funeral staff stood. Still no rain fell. Para, McCullough, and Marcus stood near the back of the tent, alternately surveying the sky and the ceremony, and shuffled from foot to foot. The minister read again those familiar words, some sounding louder than others, that seemed to oscillate resonantly within the sad, enclosing milieu of the burial ground; "Let not your hearts be troubled … in my father's house are many mansions … that where I am you may be also." Having finished these passages, he began an informally and carefully worded obituary that told how God, who had sent the boy to brighten his parents' lives and share their pilgrimage on earth, has called little William home. He appended the ultimate consignation, "earth to earth, ashes to ashes, dust to dust."

Para spoke to Marcus out of the corner of his tight-lipped mouth: "Boy, I wish that long-winded preacher would hurry his ass up."

The minister began a prayer. It was said, but much of it was lost to the thunder. Marcus looked at his feet, kept his eyes open, never quite sure if it was somehow wrong to bow his head when he did not really belong to the grieving, reverential crowd. He was part of the work crew. "Amen." The minister walked around the grave to stand between it and the heaving family, offer final words of condolence, and shake hands. Para and Jack edged forward, and people began slowly to shift about, to begin to start away to the cars outside the cemetery. Lightning struck, not far away. Another bolt followed at about the same distance. Para and Jack went to the family, to get them to the funeral car. The minister bent to the mother, his ear near her mouth, and then came up to them. "Mrs. Shulze wants to have one last look at William," he said.

Para spoke in a barely audible voice to keep the conversation from the family. "The body is in pretty bad shape, Reverend," he said, "and out here in the daylight it will look a lot worse than it did in the church."

The minister nodded and went back, bent over, and talked to the mother. She stood up and approached, standing squarely in front of Para and Marcus, and said calmly, "I want to see my baby again." Her eyes were wide and dry and red. Only a handful of people remained now, waiting under the tent behind the family. Para motioned to McCullough and the two of them went up, stiffly, to open the casket. Marcus moved up beside them, and saw with some relief that no colored leaks had soaked the pillow nor run from the ears. The body looked all right, and the other two men were probably thinking the same thing and wanted to get going before the weather broke.

Marcus' sensed something, felt a new force in the sky. It came in those brief seconds while the casket lid was being raised and became known to all at the same instant. There was a thrashing, unpleasant sound. Marcus looked to the south. The shock wave of the wind was bending the distant treetops toward him like a giant breaker. The storm was upon them! Big drops of rain and balls of ice began to pop on the tent, and the wind shoved its way into the cemetery with the noise of a swift subway train pulling into a station. Hail and rain fell in white, horizontal sheets, and the tent pulled and tugged at its tethers, rattling and shuddering with the blast. The casket's floral spray and the flower arrangements atop the mound went flying about like dry leaves, and the folding chairs were blown over. Water poured off the tent roof and ran through the grass under the tent, and hail bounced on the ground and shattered on the headstones, giving a crack like the report of a .22 bullet. For a moment, Marcus had forgotten the affairs at the grave. He looked back to the casket, and his brain, his mind, swerved inside his head. The mother had taken her baby from the casket and held him to her chest. She spoke softly to him and kissed his swollen face. The rain blew onto them and little streams of the child's makeup washed onto her dress and the wax from his broken skin fell away. The father was pleading and coaxing her to put the boy back. McCullough tugged gently at her elbow, but her strong grasp held fast, and she would not relinquish her son. Marcus was soaked and felt shaky and weak. Para opened the entire casket lid instead of the half lid and stood, steadying it in the wind, waiting to receive the boy. Minutes passed, then the mother tenderly laid the little one in his bed and smoothed his hair as she had so many times while he slept. She smiled at him and patted his chest. "Goodnight, honey. Sweet dreams," she said and turned to walk away. Para closed the coffin. With the snap of the latch, the mother hesitated and seemed to stumble. The smile vanished, and her hand flew to her mouth, her face transforming and twisting into a picture of terrible pain and emptiness. She screamed, a high-pitched siren sound. Not even the battering of the ice and rain could muffle its piercing intensity. Now she knew, she really knew, that her little boy was gone forever. She had nurtured and embraced him for two years, he had played peek-a-boo and games of mischievous hiding, and he always came back. He was gone, in The River, but he came back again to Mommy. This time, though, she knew.

⪧ 16 ⪦

The angling shadows across the backyard and the rising sonority of vibrating cicadas in the live oaks that shaded it signaled the approaching dusk of another hot day. Marcus had just returned. He was now enrolled in a laboratory physics course in summer school, only a slight interruption that Frank allowed him in what was meant to be a full-time job with twice the salary.

An ambulance call from the highway-patrol dispatcher told of an accident, "a bad one," out on the northwest highway, about five miles beyond the city-limit sign with its "Friendly City of Oil and Cattle" sobriquet. From the cloud of black smoke Art and Marcus saw on the horizon, they expected, and were not deprived of, the worst.

A gasoline truck lay on its side, surrounded by white-hot fire that rose up and fell, only to rise again as new oxygen and fuel flowed into it. Flames seemed to pour from all of it, the cab, the tires, the main tank, the saddle tanks. A few dozen yards behind the truck, through the screen of shimmering heat and thick smoke, the mangled remains of two vehicles were fused into a singular sculpture of metal and glass, a mound that moved in willowy profile against the setting sun. A highway patrolman motioned for them to circle the wreck, and shouted through the window in a husky, bold voice that registered his never having seen such horror, "Pull around, through the ditch there, and along the fence! There are people who need you real bad over yonder! Don't worry about that guy there! He's already gone!"

Marcus looked forward to the ditch where he pointed, and saw, for the first time, a still-smoldering body. Arthur rammed the ambulance through the ditch and squeezed along the fence line, scraping the gold and red McCullough-Shepherd Funeral Home lettering from the ambulance side onto the posts, trying to purchase clearance without getting too close to the blazing truck.

"Lord, have mercy. Lord, have mercy," the man said. "Help my wife and baby. I cain't do nothing with these arms." He made a partial gesture to the first car, both arms dangling at queer angles between wrists and elbows. The woman was twisted at the waist, her hips at an odd, unnatural angle, her body halfway out of the car door. Her eyes were open, but she made only a low moaning sound and used no words as the crew moved her from beneath the dashboard onto the cot. They hurried to the ambulance.

"My baby is in the back seat," the man said.

The baby lay on the floor between the seats, its brain matter having fallen from a skull that had ruptured like an overripe cantaloupe dropped from a height. Marcus wrapped the child in a sheet and placed it on the ground. A teenager in the second car was dead and disfigured, and the second, unconscious, struggled to breathe, thorax heaving with loud snorting gasps and the unmistakable sounds of a crushed chest, while sparkling fragments of glass, imbedded in the dried blood on his face, looked, in the low sun, like bizarre sequins glued there. Marcus and Art put him aboard the ambulance on the second cot, and helped the man with the broken arms into the front seat. He shook his head again, and said, "Lord, have mercy." There was no room for Marcus in the little Chevrolet panel that was used for the emergency runs. Art said in a hurried, strained voice, "You stay, Slim. I'll radio home and tell them to bring the coach." He floorboarded it around the wreck and soon was gone, the siren howling into the east.

Bystanders stood in a circle, talking among themselves, straining and stretching to see the carnage, to get a glimpse inside the vehicles at the grotesque postures of death that always fetched such curiosity. Marcus felt conspicuous, blood on his clothes, unsure of his role now that he was alone. The fire trucks were there, on the other side of the tanker, men watching as the fuel burned itself out. He went to the burned body, the driver, who had almost made it. After the truck had jackknifed and skidded onto its side, it looked like he had bailed out and started to run, but the fireball and liquid caught him in the ditch and rolled over him with its pyroclastic tide, and he was about six feet short of the boundary where the burned grass ended and survival began.

"Do you know how this happened?" Marcus asked the patrolman who had first directed the ambulance around the fire.

Regaining his trained composure, the officer lifted and adjusted his hat and said in a voice dry of spittle, "I've heard that the boys in the car tried to pass the gasoline truck and hit the other car head on. The trucker probably saw what was going to happen, most likely whipped over, went off the shoulder, the load shifted, and he flipped. I expect the boys didn't see the other car coming because the sun was in their eyes. All I know is I hope I never see another wreck like this one. Lord, have mercy."

Para arrived in the funeral coach, and Marcus told him what they had found when they got there. As the purple evening settled and the last burning glow from the truck was extinguished and the wet, burned, oily smell filled the scene, they were allowed to move the bodies to the funeral home. Marcus turned over the Negro who lay in the shade of the ditch, only to discover that he was white underneath and that his hair, singed and short, had caused the mistake. Para and Marcus took him and the broken boy and the baby into the city, backing into the garage where Art was cleaning the little ambulance that he called "the hot shot." Para scooped the baby in one huge hand in a single motion and carried it tenderly, like a limp doll, to the preparation room, where he would embalm it for the colored funeral home. Jimmy helped bring the boy and truck driver upstairs, and Hank and Para worked long into the night. At five in the morning, the hospital called to say that the boy's companion had not made it, and later still that morning, Para went to the colored funeral home to embalm the baby's mother.

Marcus would never look again into his most treasured time of a summer day, the beautiful time at the setting sun, to feel its heat, without remembering the lives that didn't continue into the pleasure and peace of the evening. He lost, too. *Kyrie eleison.*

"It was horrible, Willie," Marcus said in the afternoon. "I can't forget that poor boy struggling so hard to breathe. He never came to."

Willie looked down, shaking his head in acknowledgement and a nasal "umm, umm, umm." "Yeah", he said, "if only they had been there a few seconds earlier or later, this wouldn't have happened. The good Lord had some plans right then for those people, I guess. It's hard for us to figure out."

Marcus shot back: "I don't think God had anything to do with it. It just happened. Mathematical chance, that's all, pure mathematical probability. I don't believe in all that bullshit!"

Willie studied him and frowned. "Now hold it a goddamned minute, Slim. That's no way to talk. Hell, I see you Lutherans in church all the time, kneelin', singin' those sad hymns, prayin'. Who the hell you prayin' to, if it ain't the good Lord?"

Marcus felt a growing thickness in his throat, an enclosed and protected and yet unmistakable emotion evoked by Willie's challenge. He was reaching back into his own sadness and religious doubt, to his youth of loss, his grief, his blindsided abandonment by his mother and desertion by God, in that order. He was revisiting a kind of focal and specific pain, the way that biting into a tomato causes a mouth ulcer to hurt just as surely as it did all those times that canker sores were there before. And Marcus reacted toward death and grief the way he always did: he lashed out in anger.

"Willie, I've looked into the faces of two people, I know of, at the instant they died, one on our cot and another on the table in the emergency room. Right about then, I guess, their souls and spirits left them.

Neither one was smiling like he was going to some happy hunting ground." Marcus walked swiftly away to save himself. In his car now, his spirits sank as he drove, thinking and thinking, with either emptiness or anguish or fatigue or anger, pointed first at Willie, then no anger, nor rancor for anyone. There had to be a higher power. The incomprehensible physics of the deep universe, celestial mechanics, proved it. But there was no need for a life-stealing God in his existence right now.

⁓17⁓

Marcus awoke from a dream in his alcove, a dream in which a woman using *hoch Deutsch* spoke to him in beautiful phrases and words. He wondered who the lady was, and believed, after a while, that it was his mother. But then his mother would have not used the High German he had heard.

Frank met him upstairs just as he returned, still puzzled by the dream, from breakfast at The Texas Star. "Reel," he said immediately and with force, "keep that bathroom clean and straighten up around here. After you and Jimmy run the vacuum, empty the bag. I'm tired of this place looking like a boar's nest."

Probably, Marcus surmised, Frank had seen a drop of urine on the floor in front of the toilet, or some other trivial thing, in the bathroom the four men shared. He struggled again with a reprimand given by an authority figure and couldn't wait to talk to Hank about it, to express his irritation with Frank's demands and close supervision.

"Help me get this man dressed," Hank said while listening inattentively to the story that had brought Marcus into the preparation room. Marcus unfolded and buttoned the man's white shirt and split it down the back with scissors, did the same with the suit coat, worked the body's arms into the sleeves, and tucked everything under. Hank put the socks on, pulled the trousers up, and added the tie.

"Well, let me tell you a story", Hank began, all the while continuing to attend to the appearance of his subject. "When I was in the service, a few of us were lying around under these tents, doing nothing. There was a Sergeant Massey in charge, and he yelled at us, telling us to sit up and look alive, that the Old Man might be watching from his office. The guys griped a little bit, and nobody moved, and somebody in our detail eventually said something like, 'Oh, come on. What difference does it make? Why do we have to anyway?' Massey didn't rip into us like you'd expect him to when he heard this. No, he just simply answered, 'We do it because my little girl likes an ice cream cone once in a while.'"

"I don't get it, Hank. What did he mean?"

"Well, that sergeant had to take orders from the company commander, the Old Man, whether he wanted to or not. Some of the things he was ordered to do were probably demeaning, and he may have hated it. In the end, he could care for his family by doing as he was told. The Old Man was a captain, a helicopter pilot, and a good guy. There were times, though, you'd see some shave-tail second lieutenant, barely out of ROTC, chewing some enlisted man's ass because he had the power to do it. Some of the old cadre had been in two wars, and here they were being ordered around by a kid."

It was time to go back across The River, Marcus thought, rubbing the white, mortuary-bleached skin of his arms. He needed the fresh air and heat of the fields to restore something, to get the morning out of his system, maybe no more than to let an old acquaintance know that he was going somewhere these days. He was doing all right. In minutes the old Chrysler had him across the bridge, south of The River, and immediately down Parsifal Street, past the little worn houses and the laborers, their dirt yards with beaten cars sometimes parked there, an occasional car or pick-up jacked up or partially suspended by block and tackle from an overhead tree limb. People here bought the cheap caskets.

In this limitless black land of hay fields, corn and maize, in the shade of a big hackberry tree, he and Travis watched the short, sweating men, blackened with dirt, load the hay. Bales dropped from the rear of the moving baler, reminiscent of fecal pellets shed by caterpillars as they feed on the growth of the earth with methodical drive and unending need. Their hay hooks flashing in the hot sun, without conversation the men hooked the bales and threw them up and overhead onto the trailer with powerful measured rhythmicity, where they were stacked eight high in neat, interlocking rows by two men.

"Those wetbacks really work hard," Marcus said.

"That they do," Travis answered. "They send almost all of their wages back to Mexico. Won't look you in the eye, though. Afraid you might say something about their being here illegally and all. They work hard, especially at first. Of course, once they get Americanized, they're not worth a damn." His voice trailed off. "Man, it's hot. Do you want a soda water?"

"Yeah, thanks," Marcus nodded, and Travis dragged a cooler from beneath the pickup, handed Marcus a Dr. Pepper, and pointed to the opener tied to a string. They sat on the tailgate, and Marcus felt a certain pity for the men who labored in the sun and thick dust as the monotonous thrashing of the baler continued to generate more bales, more dragging, straining, and lifting. A faint wisp of wind, just noticeable, stirred from the direction of lowering gray clouds. The merest sniff of this new air had a humid feel that meant rain might come. The men must have felt it, too, and picked up the pace, even more sweat plastering their long, black hair to the necks beneath their straw hats. And almost exactly coincident with the first, faint, distant rumble of thunder, the last bale was picked up, and the machine was silenced until the next field was harvested on another day.

"I am familiar with hay hooks, too," Marcus said, after watching a while as the Mexicans tied the loads and cared for the equipment.

"How's that?" Travis asked.

"You know that Purina feed store just across The River?"

"Yeah, I traded there off and on."

"Well, I worked there for about four years. I don't recall seeing you come in, though. Remember Troy, that colored guy with the stutter?"

"Oh, yeah, I remember him. He'd been there for a long time already when I bought my feed there. He'd wait on me. Then I started doing business

across town with the mayor's feed store, probably about the time you started working there. That must be why I never saw you around."

Marcus continued: "The owner, Oscar Harpin, you know him, was one
of the meanest men I've ever worked for. He worked us. The minute I
slowed down, he'd send me home. The next time I'd show up, I'd work
even harder. It was just the way he treated his hands. Troy and the other
men who had families weren't treated quite that way, but when they saw
what he did to me, they stepped it up, too."

Harpin had scrutinized Marcus with a cold, placid face, the light reflect-
ing off his thick myope's glasses, his eyes made tiny by them. He put
Marcus in the feed store with cases of eggs to candle and store in a cold-
room and customers to help when they came in with additional eggs, one
of their sources of petty cash. Many had foolishly let a rooster entertain
the hens, and he returned the fertile eggs to disappointed farmers who
were counting on a little extra money that day, adding a friendly suggestion to give them to *die Klucke* for incubation. Only days later, though,
Marcus was loading and moving truckloads of hay or feed alongside Troy,
Donnell, and Alfredo, decent hardworking men of loyalty and dedication
who executed the boss's will and had not make the decision to give Marcus
such heavy lifting, but neither did they voice disapproval of it.

Troy was an easy-going, well-groomed man with a stuttering delivery
and a surprising willingness to reveal provocative intimacies, such as the
positions he chose for copulating with his childless wife. He stammered
out a story, which had gotten laughs for years, about his catching "ni-ni-
nineteen me-me-meowing" cats and beheading all of them when they
became too numerous outside the window of the room where chickens
and turkeys were killed and dressed. Donnell, with eight children and a
very heavy wife, was the self-effacing, quiet man who refused to accept a
banana or apple, so unwilling to take the risk that Marcus had stolen it.
Alfredo, the strongest of all, built low to the ground, was a reverent

Catholic who always tipped his cap as they passed a cemetery on the way into the country. Finally, Joe, not very quick, did light work and watched the office; it was easy to coax him into telling the story of his injury and his painful leg. Joe's foot had been caught in a rope, and he was dragged behind the feed-store truck as Donnell, hurrying to beat the traffic, drove across the highway to the store. When he was questioned about anything, Joe's limp became more pronounced, and looking down and sadly shaking his head, a cigarette with its long ash intact waving from his mouth, he invariably adopted a pathetic tone and said wearily, "My leg sure hurts."

From the railroad car on the siding across the way to the store to the customers, the sacks and bales moved in an endless stream, made greater by a long dry spell and the shipments of feed provided through government-sponsored drought relief. All day, six days a week, the men loaded and unloaded, each sack lifted three times and sometimes more, stacked as high as the head of a tall man, and the Harpin cash registers filled proportionally. It was a time of "high cotton"; Marcus was making seventy-five cents an hour, but still, theirs was a boss with immutable and uncharitable rules, and one day, apparently having seen Marcus buy an R.C. Cola, Harpin gave him a calculated minute, came to the back of the store where Marcus sat in a doorway watching the electric welder arcing in Mr. DeLeon's blacksmith shop across the alley. "Come with me, Reel," he said. "I'm not paying you to sit around." He said nothing as he figured Marcus' wages to the penny, wrote a check, and handed it to him. Marcus took it to mean that he was fired, and walked home, sick to the stomach, and fretted and worried the rest of the weekend. Monday, he decided to return, avoided the boss, went straight to the boxcar and began working. At midday Harpin noticed and commented, "No wonder the work is going faster. Reel is here today." That was all he said, but the message in such a quick dismissal on Saturday was unambiguous for Marcus and the others alike, and Harpin's observation that work was moving faster was validation of his shrewd, if malevolent, management policies. In the evening, when Marcus' brother picked him up, he could barely walk and sagged in the seat of the car, slumped almost double. The next morning, for the first and only time in his life, Marcus cried because he had to go to work.

Troy leading, Marcus left for Port Gillette in a separate truck, although he was not licensed to drive, but he didn't care. Thirteen and needing a few weeks of age to obtain a commercial license, he welcomed the break from the store because the drive gave him a chance to sit, and he didn't have to expend so much energy trying to hold his back straight or experience so much pain astride his spine and down his legs. He drove a dump truck that was kept around to haul maize directly from the combines to the store, where they sacked it, sewing the bags closed with binder twine and making two "ears" that were handy for lifting and moving. Almost there, Troy pulled off at a little grocery market with a side window where he could be served, and Marcus asked him to buy a can of beer. "Okay, but stay out of sight. I don't want them to see your young face." Marcus had brought a lunch of Vienna sausage and crackers, and they drove to the barn where they were to load both trucks. The irony was clear. A feed-store owner who ordered his hired hands around, always by last name, never first, early on gave Marcus freedom and responsibility before he was old enough to drive legally.

It was a glorious picnic, and he threw the doors of the truck open and let the hot wind blow through, so steadily and forcefully that the noise in his ears resembled the sounds of a panel of sheet metal being shaken to simulate thunder. As far as he could see, to the bank of thunderheads on the horizon, waves of salt grass undulated, and he felt drowsy and privi-leged to be resting without a guard in sight. Troy interrupted the scene, and for a moment Marcus felt a twinge of resentment that Troy should be seized by a deep conscience, be influenced by a boss even at that distance, but Marcus was learning that he, alone, held trouble-provoking attitudes of antagonism toward authority and that he, alone, chose to challenge rather than accept any hint of domination by an adult.

Bluestem hay was stacked about ten feet high in the barn, and with their first steps inside, it was clear that this was a dangerous undertaking.

Underneath the floorboards the unmistakable buzzing of rattlesnakes greeted them, and with each bale that they pulled from overhead, they expected to have a snake drop. Marcus extended his reach with the hay hook as he worked, assuming that the hook would be an attractive, silvery lure drawing the first strike, and gradually relaxed somewhat, remembering that a cousin had reached into a hole where the dog barked and pulled out not a rabbit, but a copperhead fastened on his finger. The cousin didn't see a doctor and never had any complications. Only once did Marcus think a rattler was nearby in the hay, judging from the direction of the sound, but they finished loading without incident and tied the cargo down with rope.

They carried the loads to a place on the other side of Guadalupe City, and the buyer stood by, watching and counting every bale being moved into his loft with an air of frugality and suspicion found in farmers, usually, and always in those who had lived through the Depression and the sacrifices of the War. Because the farmer thought the feed store might cheat, and because neither Marcus nor Troy had any reason to do this for the benefit of his boss, Marcus generated a nascent dislike for this man with a pocked face and bulbous, pitted nose. Unknown to him, Troy's feelings were growing the same way, and when the man asked, "Is it going in all right? Can you get it all in?" Troy answered with "Yeah, it's getting s-s-slick now." Marcus chuckled at his co-worker's intelligent sexual metaphor, but he was surprised that a Negro would risk offending even an unpleasant white man. Then, when the second truck had been unloaded and the last bale jammed in place, Marcus walked to the well to wash the dirt and straw and sweat from his face. As he drank from the faucet, the man shouted, "Stop drinking that water! Drinking cold water when you're hot will kill you! Get away from there!" To Troy he shouted, "Push him away, push his head away!" Troy didn't react, and Marcus, head down, not seeing the approach of the man, was knocked sideways with a rude body block for drinking tepid well water. Marcus was glad that Troy had delivered that subtle "slick" insult earlier.

They hauled truckloads of cottonseed meal, sacks still warm and giving off a nutty, edible smell, and creep feed for calves and pelleted supplements to ranches far out in the prairie, a flat and almost featureless world, except for the mesquite and huisache and creeks lined with thick groves of oak and pecan trees, to farms of black land that gave the San Antonio river its pale gray thickness and made mud as tenacious as soft tar. Kids played and chased perch in the sparkling, shallow water and ran along the sand bars of the Coleto, where, not that long before, a foolhardy Colonel Fannin had led and misled his troops to their surrender and execution by the Mexican army. Ranchers asked Marcus to have the midday meal with them in their dining rooms, and towering piles of barbecued beef, roasting ears, pots of pinto beans, and cornbread were washed down with iced tea while a Mexican cook hurried in and out to keep the revolving table stocked as the men dug in and talked business in clipped language, as if to guard against giving away too much information. Troy, Donnell, and Alfredo ate with *los vaqueros y charros* at long, noisy tables with benches and had more fun, but Marcus was not to eat with the ranch hands, although he asked Troy if he could. Troy advised him that it was not right and succinctly communicated the ideological distinction that lay between the main ranch house and the workers and bound Marcus to the former because he was white, while Troy and the others were not.

Off to the northeast they drove along the canals of the rice fields to homes of substance and comfort, and they stopped to watch the pumps that drew the water from deep wells, Waukesha diesels that had such deep booming power that Marcus could feel the air vibrate in his chest. A classmate, Herbie, rode part way and asked Marcus to swim, but he was afraid of the depth until Herbie demonstrated that he could stand, and then he found the water too cold. Above, and as far as the eye could see, strings here and there of snow geese and blue geese and sandhill cranes were beginning to come in, and off in the vanishing distances, the engines that gave the oil well jacks their nodding rhythm could be heard droning on and on, bringing such wealth that Herbie casually drove a blue Cadillac on the farm-to-market roads whenever he felt like it.

In the warehouse, alone, Marcus could also indulge in self-enjoyment, and the pleasure given by his flying hand was made all the greater by knowing that his frequent releases occurred while getting paid by a boss he perceived to be niggardly, mean, and tyrannical.

On a Friday night, a burglary occurred, and the events surrounding it brought many curious people into the feed store that Saturday. The intruders had crawled under the building, cut a hole through the wooden floor, and entered the attached grocery store through a door that was never locked. They somehow got the safe, encased in concrete, into the meat locker, where they broke it open, sending chunks of concrete flying and leading to rumors that they had deliberately thrown the material on the meat out of spite. The broken safe was quickly discovered, of course, but it was around three o'clock in the afternoon before Joe noticed the hole in the feed-store floor, so cleverly had the robbers pulled sacks of feed around it. The sheriff and a couple of men showed up, shone a flashlight into the hole, talked among themselves, and promptly left. No detective work, no fingerprints taken, no photographs, no interviews, nothing. It was not at all what Marcus expected from his remembrances of radio mysteries, movies, and books where dedicated lawmen, khaki-uniformed men with pistols on their hips, wide and evil cartridge belts and Stetson hats, collected the data, put together a story, and caught the culprit.

Autumn eased in indecisively, as it always did, and trips to transfer sacks of pecans to a buyer in the town of the Mission La Bahia became more frequent. Marcus deliberately drove past that most majestic symbol of solid durability. He drove up close and found it deserted and marveled at the view in all directions from that hilltop and the freshness of the breeze washing through. Thanksgiving was now the focus, and turkeys walked around the pens out back, waiting for those who would choose them for dinner. Marcus would hook one around the leg, ignoring the flying dust and turkey waste, and let the person feel and check the bird, knocking off a little of the price when they found the breastbone crooked. Donnell dressed them after Marcus hung them up, cut their heads off, scalded, and picked them on a primitive machine that consisted simply of a motor-driven drum with some hard rubber tubes projecting from it, whirling and lashing until the feathers were off.

The work didn't let up all day, and by late afternoon, caked with the debris of the job and worn out, Marcus had to pump the waste water from an overflowing underground cistern into a tank to dump in the boss's pasture on The River. Coming back, the noise of the truck on the gravel road and his haste and preoccupation with finishing the day's work masked the sound of the freight train that was moving parallel and passing from behind. He made a sharp right turn to cross over the tracks, and unbelievably, the train was there in the right window. Contact, as loud as a sledge on a steel plate, knocked the water tank sideways, but the truck was missed. Marcus was horrified, expecting the train to brake for some official inquiry that would cost him a job, but the train flew on, and he returned to the store from the opposite direction, quickly winched the tank up and off the truck, and asked Mr. DeLeon, the blacksmith, in a most composed, but dry-mouthed petition, to weld a new valve on, replacing the only thing ruined because it projected a foot from the back of the truck bed at the intersection of impact. Marcus hoped for Mr. DeLeon's confidentiality, but felt reluctant to ask for it, thinking that asking would bestow greater import to the damage, which, when examined afterwards, showed that only milliseconds had kept Marcus and the truck from becoming a mass of crumpled flesh and steel strewn along the tracks.

Christmas trees arrived in bundles from Canada and, hung by their tops with binder twine, created a fragrant forest of slowly revolving greenery in the unheated store as the customers passed between them. The school holidays meant extra pay, and spirits lifted above the norm for the hands, and even the full-time men were cheerful. The butcher next door, always referred to as "Mr. Frank" because no one ventured to use a complex Czech surname that was missing a few vowels, said he was going for coffee at the café, a short walk along the highway toward town. Congested and feverish, Marcus thought that coffee would help him feel better, and volunteered to accompany Mr. Frank. They hadn't gone very far when Mr. Frank said, sheepishly, that he was going for a beer. "I won't tell anybody," Marcus reassured him and had coffee while Mr. Frank drank a bottle of Pearl and spoke to the waitress in his father language with smiles and shy looks that confirmed, without translation of this foreign tongue, that he was sweet on her. Mr. Frank commuted to work from some distance and was known to have a wife and family, and Marcus was amused by the butcher's quick trips, which he surely assumed went unnoticed, out the back door to rendezvous at the café.

At home, nothing was planned, and when a sister asked a brother and Marcus if they had been Christmas shopping, they shook their heads. On a Sunday, they lay in the cornfields on the prairie as dawn began to break, shotguns loaded with Number 6 shot, and waited for geese. A honk in the distance, then string of ten or so could be seen, lower than the rest. As they set their wings to land, the brother and Marcus fired simultaneously, and three fell. As the flock rose and gained altitude, another spiraled down and, after considerable searching, was found a surprising distance away. Their Christmas fowl, tough, lean, and strong tasting, was nevertheless welcome at the table of indifference.

A little success now and then charged the boys with enthusiasm and filled their after-hunt conversations with onomatopoetic honks and quacks. They recalled how geese flew over and circled, presenting a better target at the moment when they bowed their wings to settle in and how restrained the boys were not to fire as geese came head on because the pellets were sometimes deflected off their bodies and only a broken wing would bring them down. Emmitt, a good and kind man who lived alone in a small wooden house on his ranch, let the brothers and cousin come hunting anytime, asking only that they not shoot the quail. His large blue eyes swimming behind thick magnifying lenses, Emmitt shared his most private thoughts with the three of them, telling them of his all-night adventures and survival with a German prostitute and the terrible fighting near Bastogne that left him nearly blinded by shrapnel wounds. Invalided out, he came home to find that his family had dissected the great ranch into shares that gave him a division with no oil and no gas wells, a piece of land that was almost useless for grazing or anything else.

It was on his un-wealthy property, though, where the visiting boys had their recurrent friendly interactions with this defeated man, killed the doves that he had a hard time seeing in the mesquites, picked and cooked them with rice, and shared them with him in his dark, cool cabin. Across the flat and unending prairie it was his ranch that they idolized, chose, and that offered the beauty of its expanding vistas, green mesquites, and still greener huisaches in the bright winter sun, and they could walk the rutted roads and cow trails that dropped down to the San Antonio River, where a strong wall of solid trees and gray, slow water the color of weak chocolate milk marked the limit of his land. They absorbed it all. Holding onto willows on the slick banks, they set out throw lines baited with chicken guts, each line weighted with a pipe elbow to hold it in the eddies beyond a fallen tree or in the cavities washed under the bank, and caught channel cats tasting of mud from the muddy river. They harvested squirrels from the ranch's pecan trees, killed the jackrabbits and swamp rabbits, and experienced a slightly nauseated feeling as they butchered a pregnant female and had its embryos spill out. They most always left their friend and the ranch with the orange Sunday sun dropping through the grass and the coolness coming on. They wanted the return trip to the ranch to come soon.

It was raw and wet and still dark when Marcus and his brother left to hunt ducks on the marshes of the more prosperous land that had been awarded to Emmitt's brother, who had given them permission to be there with a cavalier shrug and nod. Misty rain fell, and muffled their steps through the grasses and vines as they walked, almost blindly in the gray and almost imperceptible light, toward the larger ponds. The brother motioned to drop down, and they inched forward, crouching, and finally lay prone under the cypress trees, where they could just now make out the dark, swimming profiles of ducks out front. Shotgun shells were expensive, and the plans were the usual: shoot the ducks on the water. He signaled, and Marcus released the safety on his gun, the Winchester pump, and the brother raised his double barrel. They fired in unison, the brother with both barrels, and Marcus loaded another shell to intercept the birds rising from the water and the crippled ones fluttering away. A flash at his ear, a horrifying detonation, and his face was thrashed by stinging debris, his eyes burning with grit, his hearing flooded by a loud, steady ringing. "What happened? What happened?" Marcus shouted, his ears plugged with meaningless sound. Had a cherry bomb exploded in his face? The brother answered in a strange, unrecognizable voice with a terse, "The gun went off." Marcus rose, sat on the wet moss, wondering, confused, shocked.

He waded out to collect the ducks that bobbed upside down not thirty yards away. He brought them in, blue-winged teal mostly, and laid them beside the shotgun that he had dropped like a slugger's bat at the plate. The watermelon-sized hole blown into the soft soil, not more than inches from the point where a plumb bob would have indicated the center of his head, told the story of unpredictable fractions of time and space that separate the innocent from eternity. The brother had broken open the shotgun during the flurry, dropped two shells in, and slammed the breech closed, perhaps with his fingers on the triggers or maybe the gun had fired spontaneously as the barrel tips came up, both pointing toward Marcus' head, but just enough off-axis to miss at close range. Marcus was spared by an infinitely small distance under this vast morning panorama of grasses, trees, water, and a lead-colored sky that dwarfed them all.

Over the years, he would reflect many times on his close brushes with death as he saw others lose their lives when fractions of time or space would have spared them.

⇒ 18 ⇐

Twice Marcus radioed the police dispatcher for the nature of the emergency, and both times he was informed that it could be a gunshot wound. As he approached the house, the prolonged, bellowing groan of a man could be heard, and it was with some uneasiness that he and Jimmy entered the living room. On the bare wooden floor, in the middle of the brightly lit room, a man lay on his back, propelling himself with his heels and raised knees, his shoulders pressed flat, rotating in a circle as if a spike had been driven through his chest into the floor. About halfway around each turn, he groaned aloud; a pink, watery fluid pooled beneath him, not bright red, but giving off the unmistakable metallic smell of blood. The wall was splattered with blood and tissue, the left side of his chest was stripped of flesh, and where the biceps of the left arm had been, only a thin bridge of muscle remained along the humerus, white and exposed. Leaning against the corner was the shotgun that caused this, but the man, through hesitation or reluctance or a simple miscalculation, had fired into himself at so great an angle that he only lost the chest wall and arm muscle and thus remained with us.

He made low, moaning sounds as they loaded him into the ambulance and then remained quiet, except for his hoarse breathing, as they drove in.

Somehow, Marcus knew that the loud, booming utterances he had generated in his home, in front of his wife and all of them, including the police, were not to express his emotional agony or the bleeding pain he had caused in his torn flesh; he was growling, in defiance, with undirected internal anguish, informing the assembly that his self-destructive act was incomplete. They would be back at that address some day. About this, Marcus was sure.

Time and days had moved on, and it was four o'clock in the morning. Hank and Marcus were back in the same living room, now decorated in warm colors and softened with an oriental rug. The bedroom, though, was splashed in the most obscene way with the brain matter and blood of the man, flopped sideways on the bed, little remaining above the base of his skull and protruding, sightless eyes after the same 12-gauge they had seen before finished its gory work. What unforgivable cruelty to his wife, knowing she would rush in after the gun exploded and see him, this horror, a lifetime nightmare. She stood now, pale and wasted, in the middle of the living room, her fingers knotted together, motionless except for the occasional feral rolling of her eyes toward the room where the dead man lay. It made Marcus sick. It wasn't the bits of skull and brain that he tried to scrape off the walls, the deep black-red clot pooled at the remains of his head, the smell of the shotgun's destruction—it was the deep revulsion he had for someone who would scar another so viciously. Hank and he took the man to the funeral home, and checked the time. Barry's Café was open all night, so they went across The River to breakfast. Marcus couldn't eat. He drank coffee. They sat without talking as the light of dawn grew. Finally, Hank said, "I'd better get on with my miserable work."

It was good being back now, home, in the chemical smell of the upstairs and away from the revolting texture of that early morning. Marcus changed and went to his eight o'clock class, still angry, still angry. He hated suicide.

But it turned out, it followed him, just days later, to a different place with different people.

A short, thin woman with a passive face met them in the driveway. "My husband is on the back porch," she said, not taking her hands from her apron pockets.

"What's the matter with him?" Marcus asked.

She didn't change expression. "He's around the back. You can go around the side of the house."

Marcus took the handle at the foot of the cot and led the way, ducking under the clothesline tied between two chinaberry trees and parting the faded sheets and animated work clothes that flapped almost horizontally in the wind, and dragging the cot through tall grass that had not been mowed for a long time. Now it was apparent who had lost interest in cutting the grass. "My God," Jimmy said. "Look at that."

There, hanging from a double strand of baling wire, was the husband. He really did want to die, and had picked a most grotesque mechanism to end it all. He had disconnected the chain from a porch swing, tied the wire to the hook in the ceiling, stuck his head through a half-hitch loop while balancing somehow on the armrest and back of the half-slung swing, and then probably kicked himself free, to strangle in a slow and most agonizing way. He dangled there, swaying slightly, turning in slow motion like the four ball pendulum suspended in a crystal-domed brass "anniversary" clock, with the steady wind from the marsh raising a sweet sibilance through the salt cedars and the screen wire that surrounded this unreal scene, bringing a fishy smell.

"We can't take him down, Jimmy," Marcus said, and went back to the front of the house, where the woman remained, motionless. "Did you call the sheriff's office?" She shook her head. "May I use your phone?" She nodded, and added, "It's on the kitchen table." Marcus called the operator and was connected. A deputy took the information down. He called the funeral home.

"Frank, we have a death. Who can come?"

"I'll send Hank. He knows his way around Nueces. Gimme the directions."

The wait for the sheriff and the county justice of the peace gave Marcus a chance to look around. The little house stood alone, bleached and peeling, at the end of a narrow road paved with oyster shells that snaked back and forth through tall cattail reeds and grasses. Except for some wet coffee grounds spilled on the counter, the place looked restful and refreshing, with views of the tidal flats in almost every direction, where the trills of redwing blackbirds through the open windows were loud and frequent, and clear spaces reflected the humid sun off the choppy patches of water. Through the curtains, white chiffon restlessly rising, twisting, and settling again, he watched the woman taking the clothes off the line, tucking the sheets under her chin and folding them neatly. She stacked the things on the gallery, and stood, still and expressionless, her back toward the house, looking up the road expectantly.

The men were given the go-ahead to take the man down. Jimmy and Hank wrapped their arms around him and rose up. Somebody from the sheriff's office brought a chair over, an officer climbed up to slip the wire garrote over the man's head as they strained to hold him steady. It was difficult. The wire, cinched deep into his neck and throat, couldn't be grasped. Leaning over, reluctant to touch the body, the officer couldn't reach the hook. They eased back down, and the dead man's weight returned to the noose with an audible creak from the ceiling. He turned a little, more this time like the Christmas trees that had hung by their necks in the feed store a long time before. The deputy left, came back with a pair of pliers, and with a subsequent lift, cut the wire about halfway down. They laid the man on the cot, tucked the ends of the wire under and covered him, and took him to the ambulance. With a brief, sideways glance in their direction, the woman talked to the sheriff and the justice of the peace, her back to the white dust of departure up the road, her hands in her apron pockets.

The funeral home buried him among the salt cedars and those other families sleeping side by side outside of the little town, in the bald land where only token patches of grass held on and the sea breeze and summer squalls had already claimed before what soil they could. The same gentle wind that morning added musical, shadowy sounds to the ceremony as it moved through the trees, trees that grew with their limbs turned from the sea toward the mainland in submission to the inexorable pressure from the wind and water. Marcus took greater interest than usual in this funeral, having been there from the first through the ending, as if he had a personal stake in it. He listened again to the voice of the minister as it rose in the air, pleasing to hear in the openness. "In my father's house are many mansions; if it were not so, I would have told you. I go to prepare a place for you. And if I go and prepare a place for you, I will come again and receive you unto myself, that where I am, there you may be also."

They ate in a café on the main street. Dressed in dark suits, Para, Jack, and Marcus attracted more than one curious look in this town of deep-brown shrimpers and informal cattlemen, but no one asked questions or made any remarks about the event that all knew of.

Marcus had never had a more delicious dinner of chicken and dumplings, nor did he ever find out what tortured, internal agonies had passed between these two, driving the one to kill himself in a way designed so that both must suffer such rending pain and so his wife should always have that image of the porch in her mind. She seemed indifferent and dry-eyed at the funeral. Marcus never went down that oyster-shell road again.

⁓19⁓

"Willie! Willie! Come with me! A man's been shot down on the Lane, and nobody's here to go with me." Willie stood at the back fence of the funeral home, talking to James, Mrs. Buchanan's chauffeur, on the other side.

"I can't do that," Willie answered emphatically. "You know the bosses'll get mad at me if I do. They would naturally chew my ass good. You'd better call somebody."

"Oh, just come on, Willie. I don't have time to wait for that," Marcus persisted. Willie climbed in, and the little ambulance sailed down Dutch Lane and stopped in front of a beer joint not more than half a mile from the funeral home.

"What do I need to do?" Willie asked.

"Just take that end of the cot and help me roll it in. I don't know what we're getting into."

People were crowded inside, talking in excited voices, staring at a man who lay sprawled on his back, not a mark on him, not moving, not breathing. "He may not be dead," Marcus said to Willie. "Let's load him and go." Marcus wasn't thinking that a glimmer of life might have remained in this man; he thought there must still be a gunman in the place, someone filled with beer and remorseless anger who had an interest in the ambulance crew and the man on the floor.

"Where the hell are the cops?" Marcus asked, as they lifted the heavy, limp figure, arms dangling, with difficulty, and rolled him, awkwardly, onto the cot. A shout stopped them short. "You leave that man right where he be. That's what he gets for foolin' with my woman." Marcus didn't see a pistol, only a dark man, bigger but not taller than he, approaching the cot and Willie. Willie watched him, a flicker of concern changing his face, and Marcus sensed a code of understanding that passed between the two, as they stood almost face-to-face. For Willie, who had "dipped his wick in foreign oil" on many occasions, and maybe into the wife of this drunk murderer, it was a silent recognition and acceptance of a violent crime that sometimes happened in his end of town. Sounds at the door and outside told them during that frozen moment that the police had arrived. "Everybody back against the wall!"

On the examining table in the emergency room, the man's shirt was open. The doctor pointed with a hemostat at the mole-sized hole, from which not a drop of blood oozed, on the left chest. "It just clipped the aorta," he said. "Fraction of an inch either way, he might have made it. Must have been a .22 short. Didn't come out the back."

Willie was quiet and pensive on the way back to the home. Marcus knew that he was troubled, not by having handled a warm body of someone so recently killed, but by that look from the shooter and the message of triumph that it conveyed. It was less than a day later. Willie had the second, older lowering device scattered in pieces on the garage floor. "It's not working for some means," he said.

"Do you know what the matter is?" Marcus asked.

"No," he said again, with a note of irritation in his voice. "It's not working for some means, contrary goddamn thing that it is." Willie was not happy. He lit a cigarette.

They sat on the tailgate of the pickup out back. Neither spoke. Marcus finally shrugged and said, "You know, Willie, that man that was shot last night didn't amount to much in his life, did he?"

CHAPTER NINETEEN

Willie removed his cigarette and bluntly denied a presumed assessment by Marcus of a Negro's value, choosing to speak about the dead man in the present tense. "His skin may be dark, but his blood is just as red as yours, Slim."

"You're right, Willie. You're right."

They were silent again for a few minutes. Willie took a deep breath. "I will never understand Niggeroes," he said. "That man who shot the other guy doesn't even have much of a pecker they tell me. The story I hear is that he got it infected in the army after he made some whore mad and she bit him. He was too scared to go to the medics, scared of a court martial, waited too long, had to have it operated on, I think, and his dick ended up all crooked and scarred. That poor bastard practically has to squat to piss. He couldn't do much with his woman, and he just didn't want anybody else to do it either." Marcus could envision the sexual act that led to the dead man's injury in Korea, and then, knowing he had no right to ask it, he did ask another question, nevertheless, hoping that his friend would confide in him, appease even more his prurient curiosity.

"Willie. Did you ever poke that man's wife?"

"No", he said, not looking. "I never did. I wanted to, though. That just as easy coulda been me on that floor."

Willie sighed again. "I'd better put this gimbelly-assed lowering device back together."

Marcus rose to return to the office, hearing Willie's loud exclamation behind him as he walked up the steps, "Work, you *chingadera*, work!

Edith, the part-time receptionist, emerged from the ladies' room. Marcus was feeling older, manly among men. "Hey, Edith. Is your soul full of hope, or is your hole full of soap?" The men laughed. Dietz frowned. "Don't talk that way, Slim. And stop calling Edith 'Satchel Butt,' too." Edith looked angrily at Marcus.

Para walked in, and Marcus knew that much more was coming. Para was red-faced, and he looked older and more authoritarian. His thin lower lip, usually tucked under, was now bitten totally underneath. He took his glasses off and rubbed the bridge of his nose. Marcus saw a different, unusually reflective glare in Frank's uncovered brown eyes. He laced into Marcus. "What the hell is wrong with you, Reel? Don't ever take Willie on an ambulance run again. What will people think if they saw you?"

The words stung Marcus and hurt his feelings, all the more so because there were witnesses nearby in the office. He answered, subdued. "I thought it would be all right, since it was down on the Lane."

"Come again?" Para said in a rising voice. "You just don't make ambulance calls with Willie. That is not his job."

Marcus knew that Para was right, and the neighboring funeral home would have enjoyed spreading jokes all over town about the composition of the ambulance crew, but deep inside and after the fact, Marcus also knew that the only person who could have profoundly absorbed the events in that bar at that moment and could translate them for him didn't have a white face like his.

$\backsim 20 \backsim$

A cluster of agitation in the empty lot behind The Post Drive-In Café could only mean one thing: a fight at lunchtime. In the center, in the bright school-day sun, Bobby Fox and Joe Moring circled and taunted, neither willing to be first to engage the other. Bobby was the aggressor and more fearsome, a short, stocky boy with a perpetual, mean scowl and an attitude of absolute indifference toward anyone, teacher or principal alike, a troublemaker with long, greasy hair to match, and a face made more sinister by the confluence of his eyebrows, connected at a vibrissae-like point on the bridge of his nose and angling up from there, giving him the look of a demonic jack-o'-lantern. Joe was the more muscular combatant, handsome, dark-haired, and he probably had an advantage in strength, but his darting eyes and hard swallows betrayed his nervousness. He, like Marcus, was afraid of Bobby, by reputation if not by fact. He stumbled, and Fox flew into him, pounding his face and causing a thin trickle of blood to flow from his nose. Joe let go with a kick aimed at the groin and fell. Bobby kicked him in the mouth, and Joe jumped up, fists raised, even more fear on his bloody face and now engorged lips. Bobby boasted, "Now I'm really gonna whip your ass," and for the first time, Marcus felt sorry for Joe, himself a schoolyard tyrant and a kid feared by many. Joe took a big swing, propelled by endocrinal fright and rage, and caught Bobby high on the cheek, a quick pop that lifted the receiver's wavy hair and knocked him backwards. The fight was over. One said to the other, "It's settled then?" "Yeah," the other replied.

True to his lifestyle and reputation, Bobby never lived into the later days of adulthood. Killed in an out-of-town car wreck that left his face mutilated, he had just been embalmed and placed in a closed casket in the back chapel.

Marcus sprawled across the sofa near him, notes and papers spread out in a fan shape on the floor. He worked at physics problems without looking up as Hank appeared with Willie in the doorway. "We just about screwed up royally today, didn't we?"

"I'm telling you," Marcus answered, closing his slide rule.

"What do you think, Willie? Did you see what happened? I wonder if the family saw anything?" Hank questioned Willie about that afternoon's disaster.

Willie was scraping and working at a vanilla ice cream cup that he had bought across the street. He licked the lid and stopped chewing the wooden spoon to answer. "I didn't see much. I was lookin' the other way at the time, I guess." The three talked for a while about it.

"We'd better mention it to Jack and Art in case anything comes up," Hank concluded. "Shorty might say something about it, too. Frank had his back to the grave, but he said that he didn't think anybody was looking at us when it happened, that the minister was talking to them."

It was a troublesome event in an otherwise routine funeral.

Marcus never knew Shorty's real first name. No one ever used it, as if indeed he had none. Shorty paced on runty, fat legs that afternoon, looking into the distance up the highway to Guadalupe City. He shaded his eyes and looked again. The sun reflected off the silky sheen of his cheap

Dacron suit, and sweat wrinkled his collar. He pigeon-toed, wiping the dust off his shoes on the backs of his trouser legs. Sweat poured from his face, round and red. Finally, he was relieved of his wait. "There they come." Headlights shimmered through the heat, some distance away, and the procession gradually came into view.

Shorty wasted no time getting to the cemetery office just beside the entrance. He jumped over a low hedge, and his bantam legs carried him to the other side like a duck landing on water. The chimes started "Rock of Ages." Willie took the pickup away and removed his hat respectfully. Marcus again checked the gravesite and the few flower sprays placed there that broke the monotony of a flat green lawn where the dead lay in neat rows marked by recessed bronze markers that allowed lawnmowers to roar over deliberately unimpaired. He met Hank and the pastor at the lead car that brought the newborn in her tiny pink casket to this carillon serenade and her rest in Babyland at the rear of Memory Gardens. Para's car came up behind them, and Para opened the doors of the family limousine, hot engine left running, air conditioning trying to win against the sun beating on the vehicle's black body.

The minister walked toward the family, and Hank took the casket. Marcus was at his shoulder. They had gone about thirty or forty steps toward the grave when the unthinkable happened. Holding the casket at the ends as an adventurer would present a chest of jewels to a foreign king, the weight of it imperceptibly transferring to the heels of Hank's hands, the latch on the lid gave way and the casket dropped away, swinging on its hinges, suspended from the lid gripped in Hank's hands. The baby fell to the ground. In a frantic instant, Hank scooped her into the satin box again, bits of grass flying with her. Shaking, he looked back. The family was still gathered in a group at the cars. "I don't think they saw me. I don't think...." They had heard too many stories of lawsuits, the mental-anguish kind, initiated by acts as trivial as an embalmer's pulling a hair from a facial mole in front of a family member who requested its extraction, or a tiny bubble revealed, purging from a body's mouth, when a careless attendant opened a casket without first clearing the room of observers. Apparently no one behind had noticed the baby's fall or did not care why the men knelt and arose so hurriedly. Shorty saw. He breathed deeply, looked down, shook his head sympathetically, aware of the predicament should the issue surface later.

But the service ended, and they gave the infant to the land, sleeping face down, and without spoken agreements or more discussion, the four witnesses, including Willie in the pickup, never mentioned the event again. Ironically, Shorty had already made plans to leave Guadalupe City and dropped out of sight soon afterwards, moving to Arizona because his wife had some kind of respiratory ailment.

⁓21⁓

In the ditch, in the dark, Marcus and Hank pulled the dead man from the wreck. "Looks like he straightened out that curve," Hank said, looking up the highway. "Must have been in a real hurry."

At the embalming table, Para pulled the bloodied trousers off, and Marcus prepared to stuff them into a paper sack. Crumpled bills, many of them, fell to the floor. "*Chingada,*" muttered Marcus. The man's wallet had been kept by the authorities, but no one had apparently searched the man's pockets, and now Marcus did that, having never really wanted to know what lay in any dead person's pockets before then. Mostly ones and fives, some tens, the treasure came to over four hundred dollars or, in terms of a student's life, a modest fortune. Marcus counted out loud.

"Put it in the safe," Para instructed. "When the family comes, we'll give it to them."

"I wonder where it came from?" Marcus asked.

"Most likely he robbed a store or something. That's why he was driving so fast."

Marcus did as he was told, muttering to himself as he locked the safe downstairs with silent shrugs that his and Para's honesty had separated him from what amounted to four months of school-year salary.

Two people, Para and Marcus, knew of the cash in the dead man's pockets. The one who had gotten this unidentified money, yet to be inherited by a family ignorant of its existence, was embalmed. There were no inquiries by the police, no questions of booty from a robbery, no news of holdups. No one visited the body after a sister came to pick out the casket. The man was a drifter with no fellows at a job who missed him, no church members talking of his goodness, no neighbors who spoke of his flourishing avocado trees and elephant ears. And then, as Marcus watched *Gunsmoke* alone on that Saturday evening, three men came and asked to view the body. Marcus showed them the register, still blank, but they didn't sign it, and he led them to the back chapel. Were they investigators? They came back to the office after a few moments and looked around inquisitively, behavior that was clearly different from that of the usual mourners. Marcus stood with his back to the desk.

"Was he dead when you picked him up?" the one asked.

"Yes."

"And you, uh, brought him straight back here?"

"Yes."

"What happens to the stuff in his pockets?"

Instantly, Marcus knew that these visitors had a reason for that question. They must be on the track of the four hundred-plus dollars. Marcus hedged. "I think the highway patrol keeps it until the next of kin is notified. That's all I know." They didn't move.

Another stepped forward slightly, started to speak, then said to the others, "Let's go." It was an unsettling experience, and Marcus sat down to think about responses that withheld information. At arm's length was the safe holding the loot that they had apparently wanted. How did it come to be stuffed in the pockets of a derelict who drove too fast for the Port Gillette highway?

At the graveside, the denouement that Marcus had sought was played out with only the sister and her young child, the funeral home employees, the *ad hoc* Presbyterian minister who came when asked, wearing his customary cowboy boots, and the old retired fellows recruited to be pallbearers in situations like these. The service was generic and soon over.

Marcus liked this particular bearded and athletic clergyman. He was direct and gave his message succinctly. Most of all, Marcus appreciated a minister who did not assume that he was lovable, one whose conversation was not sprinkled with happy and church-inspired platitudes intended to make others believe that he was entitled to goodness. They talked as Mora prepared to close the grave, and a tall man, taller still than Marcus and wearing a white linen suit with a red string tie, came up behind. He had been a classmate of Marcus in junior high and a year beyond and, rumor had it, had dropped out to become a professional gambler in Hot Springs or Galveston or Nevada. Someplace. Marcus and he shook hands, his soft and cold.

"Did you know him, Bobby?"

"Yes, I saw him a few times," he answered, preferring, apparently, not to enlighten Marcus further. "I didn't know much about him, though, really."

Bobby stayed, watching the men shoveling the dirt into the grave for a few minutes, then left with a wave of a hand. So that was it! The money, Marcus now suspected, had been accumulated in a poker game and ratholed as it was won, leaving the players at the table without a gambling gentleman's means of properly assessing his losses or regaining them. Maybe he had cheated—possible but unlikely with players of that caliber in games with such high stakes. Most likely he had been very fortunate that evening, left the table too soon, and drove too fast, too drunk with whiskey or euphoria to negotiate a quick curve. Bobby, and the three men who came to the funeral home the Saturday evening before, had indeed come to pay tribute to a card player who, although he had broken the rules of the table by cramming money into his pants pockets as he went along, had died because he couldn't handle his accomplishment. Those three men didn't come for the money that had been lost after all. They were there to pay respects because each knew that a gambler with good luck always runs out of it.

⁓22⁓

Para and Marcus answered a call from a shocked witness to murder. "Somebody's been shot! Hurry, hurry!" she screamed into the phone. Siren on, they sped to the restaurant, pulled near the small knot of people and police cars, and brought the cot forward. They stopped and stood near the vehicle.

A man snapped at them with a justified invective, "What are you standing around here for? You're nothing but a bunch of vultures."

Para answered simply, "We're here to help if you need us," and edged back.

The man's mother lay face down on the sidewalk in front of the restaurant door; his stepfather sat in the police cruiser, surrounded by officers and onlookers. "Do you have something to cover her with?" the man looked at Marcus, his voice cracking, "For God's sake, cover my mother up!" Marcus moved toward the cot, but Para put his hand on his arm.

"Let the police take care of it. They have to take pictures and do some other stuff."

The officers emerged from the cruiser, the stepfather in handcuffs.

"You sonafabitch, you sorry sonafabitch!" The man lunged toward his stepfather and was restrained by a circle of police. He roared, shaking with tears of rage, pain pouring down his reddening face.

CHAPTER TWENTY-TWO

The pathologist came into the quiet of Para's preparation room and began his autopsy. Taking a probe from his bag, head tilted back to look through his bifocals, he began to trace the paths made in the torso of the woman by the .38 caliber bullets. Five entrance wounds: four in the front, one in the back. He talked to his tape recorder and opened the chest and abdomen, continuing to describe the penetrations and bleeding, stopping now and then to snip a piece of tissue that he dropped into a small Erlenmeyer flask of clear fluid or bending down to peer at some anatomical structure through the loupe he wore above his glasses. Finally, taking off his rubber gloves with a self-satisfied smile, pleased with his analysis and sharing a conclusion borne confidently out of his experiences, he said, "She would have survived the four bullets from the front, but the one in the spine killed her. She must have been shot one last time, in the back, after she had fallen forward."

The son came to make the funeral arrangements. Marcus thought he knew him, or his name anyway, from somewhere. Slowly, he reassembled the pieces. It wasn't the grieving son who Marcus remembered—it was his mother on the embalming table. She had a different name now, having taken that of her murderer-to-be in matrimony. She was the woman in the trailer house on Parsifal Street who took Marcus to Mrs. Sattler's house when the father needed a doctor for his pneumonia, she who smoked cigarettes without removing them from her lips and wore a bra without a blouse, inside and outside the aluminum trailer. It was her half-Mexican baby that Mrs. Sattler had brought to the house one day, the little boy's face deeply bruised by a fist, a blow from her or a Mexican boyfriend, no one was sure, but Mrs. Sattler was sickened by it and shook her head sadly, knowing she would have to return the baby to his mother for more of the same. The woman on the table didn't look the same in death—people never did—but the man who picked out the casket had a familiar face because Marcus had seen him once or twice around the trailer, a son from a liaison long past. The body was ready for viewing, and the man now sat in the office afterwards, voice trembling and husky with sadness. Then he composed himself, smoking in quick, rapid puffs, one crushed out, another lit. Marcus asked him about the little half-Mexican half-brother. Where did he go?

"You may remember the man who was living with my mother at the time?"

"Yes. He had a bad leg. He took me fishing a few times on the Guadalupe, and he seemed to walk with a lot of pain, I remember. I liked him. He showed me how to fish. I can still hear him, telling me to set the hook, not to hurry. It was such a temptation to yank that line right out of the water with the first nibble."

The man nodded. "He did have lot of pain. He had been burned on electric wires, and it didn't heal, and he always had this open sore. Well, one day, he took off, and took the boy with him. I never heard from him again. He was really a good guy and wanted to marry my mother, but she refused. Then, about five or six years ago, my mother married this guy who killed her. I don't know why he shot her; I think they were going through a divorce or something." His voice became phlegmatic.

Marcus looked at the man, well-spoken, articulate, respectfully referring to the deceased as "my mother" even when she was lying prostrate, arms splayed outward in a pose of crucifixion, on the sidewalk. "She called me yesterday morning from the café where she worked, and told me she was afraid of her husband because he had a gun and had threatened her. Could I pick her up when she got off at four? Her husband must have been waiting for her outside, and when she went out front to wait for me, he killed her. It happened about fifteen or twenty minutes before I got there. The police had already arrested the bastard; he didn't even try to run away."

And so the life of the lady in the trailer closed. She had driven a kind, suffering man to take that forsaken and beaten half-caste waif somewhere to a better life, but she had also produced a good and caring son who loved his mother. In the end, paradoxically, it was the fifth and last bullet that elevated her from the umbra of a whore's underachieving life so that Marcus could see her last and meager contribution after all.

~23~

Jimmy's friend from Galveston, Louis, a year or two older, came to spend a few days. The three talked about going to a whorehouse, and Marcus knew he had to be initiated soon or he would never defeat the superior positions that the other two held over him, their having had sex, nor would the recurring bumps on his face go away, according to Jimmy, until he joined their thus-privileged membership, nor could he have peace until he knew what copulation was like. They pointed the car west and drove through a gray February mist and the city of the Alamo and miles of ranch land and vacant fields toward Old Mexico.

They each, in his own mind, anticipated what was going to happen. Conversations were, off and on, about sexual adventures and observations. Marcus told of his introduction to the language when the brother, in fourth grade, told him, in the second grade, that he had learned a new word, "fuff." It was an interesting word, and the definition of it was rather curious, because Marcus couldn't quite equate a urinary appendage with procreation, although he had seen things happening between animals on the farm. Jimmy and Louis laughed again when he related how that same brother had seen girls' breasts exposed and surprised couples scrambling like cockroaches at the Sky Hi Drive-In Theater as he moved briskly from car to car with a wooden crate of Cokes just before the booming lights of intermission came on.

"There was this time," Marcus added, "that we were watching some Easter play in the auditorium. This girl was wearing a homemade rabbit suit, and when she came out on the stage, you could see right through it. They should have checked that thing out in bright lights beforehand. Anyway, there she was, basically jumping around in her underwear, and you could see her black patch, or at least you thought you could. I guarantee every boy in that auditorium had a hard-on."

Louis related the story of Honest August. August was playing cards with his poker-playing buddies, who had secretly wired an electric-fence transformer to the chair he always chose. During their usual banter, someone nonchalantly asked if any of these farm boys had ever "screwed a sheep." Somebody threw the switch and August jumped up with a shout. The men howled. Since that time, he was "Honest August". The story was just as entertaining told again in the car, even more so because of the beer that catalyzed their jocularity.

Finally, they crossed the Rio Grande, and proceeded along a rough dirt-and-gravel road to Villa Acuna. After they arrived and parked, no one took notice as they hustled up the unpaved street in the early afternoon, the usual hordes of kids asking for nickels or trying to sell Chiclets weren't around because of the unpleasantness of the weather, apparently, while the same fog held and concentrated the smells of burning meat and frying *chicharrones*.

They looked into a bar, and immediately were beckoned with a loud, "Come in, come in, boys!" from the bartender. Inside it was dark, made even more so by the overcast day, and perfused by a mothball-like smell that conflicted with a subtle perfume wafting from the four or five girls who sat in booths in the back watching the trio, the only customers. They ordered beer and drank from the bottles, eschewing the filmy glasses that had been placed alongside. Louis got up, and spoke to a girl who met him on the dance floor. "Are they going to dance?" Marcus asked Jimmy. He shook his head with a wise smile. Louis disappeared with her through the backdoor. Jimmy got up, made quick contact, and Marcus followed suit and, almost quizzically, approached a young girl, probably not more than sixteen, in a simple blue dress, who asked, "You want me? Five dollar." She held up her hand, five fingers spread.

The two girls took Marcus and Jimmy through the backdoor into a dirt courtyard encircled by half a dozen attached, one-story, unpainted stucco rooms that were entered without even a step above the packed earth. Outside the door to the room an old woman wearing an off-white waitress's uniform met them, motioning toward their zippers, indicating that they should pull them down. "Now what?" Marcus thought. Was she one of the whores? The lady thrust her hand in and pulled him out, stretched the foreskin back, twisted and squeezed down like you would on a cow's teat, checked the hair, and let go. Marcus zipped up. "Twenty-five", she offered her palm. Marcus laid a quarter in it and turned to the girls, who stood at the door impassively chatting.

"Jimmy! Aren't you going to use a rubber?"

"No," he answered. "Be like taking a shower with your socks on."

"But you might catch something."

"Who gives a crap?" he continued. "I'll get a shot of penicillin if I do." With that, he stripped his pants down and tossed them toward the dark corner. It was an unreal, fast-moving scene, the girls undressing in the rose-colored light of a small lamp, lying parallel on the small bed, supine, giggling. Jimmy's bare ass rose into the air, his girl's legs opened, and with a few movements, accompanied by his muffled utterances of "Slow down, slow down, take it easy," he was done. It was Marcus' turn, and he was nervous, scared, and uncertain, hands cold and clammy, his important part still soft and withdrawn. He touched her breast; she twisted her chest away slightly and giggled, "*Frio*" and reached for the rubber that he fumbled with. She lifted him and teased it with a single fingertip, a wispy touch on an exquisite target. Marcus emptied himself in an uncontrollable instant and started apologizing: "I'm sorry, I don't know what happened."

Her midnight eyes open, he pressed his lips briefly on hers, a faint garlic smell. Then she whispered in a moment of sensitivity that stayed with him forever. "You come back. This time we do for love."

Jimmy searched in the corner and cursed, "Oh, hell! My pants fell in a bucket of water." The girl took the foot tub from him, squatted over it and performed her rapid toilet, splashed water briefly, and replaced the tub in the corner to be used after the next man and the others who would follow. Thus, Marcus' first sexual experience was short, without intromission, and had a witness, worst of all. His shame was as deep as his embarrassment. They returned to the bar, neither saying anything, and Marcus ordered refried beans and tortillas. A thin, unshaven drunk stumbled in and looked around. The girls approached him, but he waved them away with a loud, weaving laugh, adding, "I'd stick it to you, too, if I had the money."

The afternoon drifted past and the small brown bottles of beer that they liked, called Coronado, began to have the desired effect. Jimmy waltzed to a *cancion* from the jukebox, his large-mouthed companion flashing a metallic field of silver dental work as they turned. Her smile seemed like that of the little boys who stripped foil from gum wrappers and cigarette packs and pressed it to their teeth, a maneuver that in adulthood would bring fillings and bridges to life with a repulsive, blackboard-scratching shudder.

"Where did you learn to dance like that?" Marcus shouted to him.

"East Texas," he answered. "I learned it to impress the girls. They dance to that Cajun music up there. Pretty girls. Ridge runners, I call them." His brown eye and his gray eye opened wide in a happy gesture, his tobacco-stained grin ever widening. They laughed aloud with alcoholic delight, and Marcus composed a prosaic statement for them all. "You know, Jimmy, alcohol dulls the brain and causes insanity in the family."

He looked up to see a girl, the girl he had first chosen, return to the bar from the street. He approached her and said, low and into her ear, "You said you would for love". She looked puzzled at first, then smiled and took his hand, leading him to the back.

The consummation was perfect, perfect and manly, and he held her proudly, hoping to extend the pleasure of her presence and assuming that the others outside would think it meant that he had staying power, could really satisfy a woman, could give it to her until she screamed, could hold his own explosion in check. He bent near her triangle, pushed her legs yet further apart, opening her, his face washed by her tangled sexual odor. "Why are you loo-king?" she frowned.

"Because I want to see you."

She didn't understand, and pinched her mouth in a minor display of disapproval as she assumed Marcus was checking her for disease, when it was only curiosity about her treasure, one warm and living, his having seen it many, many times on the dead lying on their backs on the embalming table, like the young mother who drowned in the bay, and those genitalia were cold, lost, and meaningless. And then she was above him, rising and falling, crying "Do me some more!" and hoarse sounds came from her, vocalizations of neural joy, and long monotonic beats of soft squeals, and she lay forward on Marcus with garlic-scented, deep exhalations, ignoring his naive question, "Are you okay?" Marcus didn't know about women, and could not comprehend the reason for her grinding, writhing tension and now oblivious relaxation. It didn't connect to the same muscle-weakening spurting rhythm that had just happened in him again.

She stirred, rose, squatted over the bucket, and dressed. Without a word or backward glance, she wrapped herself in a loose gown and left. She wasn't out front when he returned to the bar, and the worn boys left to drive home in the darkening of that extraordinary day, and Marcus looked back and aside many times as they walked to the car, hoping for a glimpse of her, but it didn't happen, as if there were some mother-like significance attached to her leaving him without a goodbye.

And now Marcus was in his bed in the alcove in the funeral home, and the events of the previous day's lust replayed sweetly, pleasurably in his thoughts. He was so glad that he had been there, for now the fantasy that accompanied his private stimulation was real, and he envisioned more sex with different women. It would give him even greater fantasies to enjoy in his future. Nearby, Jimmy and Hank slept, soft snoring coming from each in perfect rhythm, first one and then the other, exactly out of phase. He held himself, and pounding blood filled everything to aching, wonderful fullness, and his finger teased that exquisite ventral spot. That spot, that morphologically insignificant point on the body that projected so acutely to the brain was the real reason for so much male behavior and so many awful misdeeds. How many fistfights and knife fights and gunfights had arisen because of it? Wars and threats and entreaties and purposeful aggression to achieve, to have, to entice, to buy, to own, to love because of it? Marcus, in his solitary bed, in a warm encirclement of windows, could only think that the Maiden of Villa Acuna knew, too, where the anatomical focus of man's body and soul lay discretely, awaiting stimulation by maybe no more than a mere thought for masculine expression to occur. Because men, like enraged bulls, must hit and strike and feel flesh give way. And even when they do not injure with weapons and fists and feet, this tiny penile field on the sexual nervous pathway to their minds will make them strut as a matador after the kill.

⟅24⟆

Marcus found many of his junior-college instructors intelligent and well-read, most of them word-loving men of a generation that preferred the spelling of "sulphur" instead of "sulfur" because it was more interesting that way. Now he was making a perfunctory effort to follow the words of the biology instructor, a thick-bodied, strong woman with a physique for women's athletics, who stood at the board discussing an illustration of the kidney. She had been mentioned sometimes in conversations by the male students in the cafeteria coffee shop, especially among the recently freed soldiers on the GI Bill who knew a lot about these things, as a woman who preferred women to men. Now she began to explain the structure and function of Bowman's capsule when a message was handed to her by an office employee. She glanced at it, and her face tightened with concern as she gave it to Marcus. The note read "Call McCullough-Shepherd Funeral Home." "It's okay," Marcus said to her. "I work there. I'll call after class."

When he called, Edith answered. "Jack wants to know if you can cut out of classes early. He needs you to go to Houston, and he wants to leave right soon."

Thus started a promising trip to pick up a body. Jack and Marcus would be able to stop for big steaks and the like because their cargo was dead and not sick, and they could stop and eat those steaks if they wanted to. The coach, at such times, would be pulled around to the back of the restaurant with the shades drawn, and even the most curious were seldom interested in a close look. Even if they did, the blue-black cot cover only vaguely suggested the features of a human being underneath.

In the Houston mortuary they waited a long time for the body to be released. The family had oil money, old wealth, and Marcus felt self-conscious and uncomfortable at first, resentful even, in the presence of these three people whose urbanity revealed circumstances in which no one had really worked very hard for a living. He struggled with his overweening distrust of them. To him, a man's character wasn't formed by successes and good things in a life only frivolously challenged, but by the failures, disappointments, and struggles he has had and by how he has risen up afterwards.

The family members took no notice of his poor underpinnings and unease though, and one or the other spoke to him with interest from time to time, asking his name and college major, wanting to know some details of his life and work in the funeral business. They were all waiting for the transport home of the woman, a respected benefactor of Guadalupe City who had the misfortune to develop cancer of the liver at a young age, was treated with heroic dosages of inhibitory drugs, and died from the stress of her affliction and its treatment. The family members following, Jack drove back to Guadalupe City without stopping. No steak dinner this time.

"Those people are well-off, aren't they?" Marcus said on the way.

"They have right smart money, no doubt about it."

Marcus wondered about Jack's feelings now. He had heard the usual jokes around town, which Jack joined into with his loud laugh. The favorite line at the Lion's Club luncheons went, "What's the definition of a hypocrite? Jack McCullough trying to look sad at a thousand-dollar funeral." Jack did seem genuinely moved by some deaths, like he did when an accidental shotgun discharge killed the hardware store owner. Other times he just seemed to be in the business of running a business. Did he consciously analyze the fact that the lady lying behind them now in the coach would have an expensive funeral, moving up to the higher-priced copper and bronze caskets and a concrete grave liner? Certainly he was glad that the funeral didn't go to the competitive funeral home. Marcus guessed that Jack didn't think of profits.

She had been a good and dignified lady and now was embraced at the viewing, the funeral service, and the burial by many friends and visitors and by a family whose habits and concerns were those of fine, sincere people, as well. Marcus felt close to her polite relatives, somehow drawn into the bond among these bereaved and kind people during those three days. These were the folks who lived in the big white houses north of The River, those homes with the high walls and iron gates that had so impressed him when he came into the town as a ten-year-old. He was strangely sad after the ceremony that late morning as he watched them file from the cemetery, knowing that it was unlikely that he and they would speak again. They departed before the grave was shoveled shut with earth, as was the usual practice because lingering to see dirt thrown into the grave of a loved one was too difficult and too final.

Marcus said very little as Willie and Dietz and he laid a magnificent panoply of flowers that spread over the new grave and some old gravesites beyond, and then, as if feeling some kind of personal connection with the deceased and her people as they returned to their homes, he took a single yellow rose from the casket spray as he left to drive the funeral coach back to the home. He placed it on the dashboard.

He stretched out on the couch in the front office with the newspaper until Jimmy's one-handed, nervous opening and snapping shut of a Zippo lighter became too annoying. With an unnoticed frown directed askance at his tormentor, Marcus left without a word.

Then he sat alone and depressed at the counter in The Texas Star. He chose to sit at the curving counter that doubled back in a kind of right turn because such a position lent itself to anonymity. Doris saw it in him and in a moment of identification and consolation by one also having a day of morose weariness said, "Let's get out of here and go for a drive in Riverside Park. Can you go now?"

"If we're not gone too long."

"Let's take my car. It's there on the street."

They sat on the bench of a picnic table with their backs against the top, watching the ripples in the slowly moving water, that same band of water that separated the poor from the non-poor. Doris sat with crossed legs, swinging one from the knee in a regular beat. The music of The River surrounded them: mockingbirds and cardinals called incessantly, and deep in the grass, crickets, always there, were now clearer, and other animal, phantom, plaintive issuances came to them, almost like an oboe's sound weaving in and out of the steady voices of a human choir. A fence lizard ran by with its jerky, spasmodic bursts. Marcus thought about it and then remembered the name they gave it as boys. A rusty gut.

"What is that sound? A frog?" Doris asked, looking up into the pecan trees, seeking the source of a glottal croaking.

Marcus answered, "No, a rain crow. A cuckoo, actually."

"Oh."

"I used to fish here. We'd set trotlines out, wade back and forth, bait the lines with grasshoppers, and run them all night long. It's only waist-deep out there. In the morning, we'd have a washtub full of catfish. It was fun. Catching those grasshoppers was work, though. We'd run ourselves through the bloodweeds until we were hot and worn out. They were big and slow yellow grasshoppers, and they were easy to cup with your hand against the stalks. Problem was, they would spur with their hind legs and spit that brown juice, and some would even bite. A brother-in-law showed me how he catches a few at a time and puts them in a mayonnaise jar with a piece of screen wire. They crawl up the sides, and you freeze the whole thing. You always have bait. Saved a lot of running through the weeds." Marcus spoke without a pause. "We'd have to watch for cottonmouths. Sometimes in the light of the gas lantern, the movements of the water looked just like a snake. Only once did one slide into the water from a snag where we had tied the line. Scared us."

He told her then of his young summer days and nights on The River when trapping minnows was about the most enjoyable experience ever handed to him. His warm memories of that episode in his life and his happiness with her at that moment flowed without containment.

She turned her face toward him as he spoke, fixed on him with eyes made even bluer by the outdoor light, nodded acknowledgement with just a suggestion of a smile that showed ever so little of her flashing white teeth. Pinpoints of sun through the brim of a beribboned straw hat moved across her face like the ballroom's globe picks up the spotlight and strafes it across the dance floor. Marcus felt a sexual avidity for her unlike any before. He wanted to touch her and kiss her. She made no motion toward him or sign that she felt the same and with an expression that seemed both impatient and churlish said, "I've got to get going."

"How come so soon?"

"I need to go home and look after the kids," she answered and started for the car.

What is she thinking about? Marcus just couldn't figure it out. Still, he was happy being near her.

⤳25⤳

It was a particularly sultry night, and Marcus was alone in the funeral home. Hank and Para were on an overnight body call, and Marcus, although welcoming the solitude and freedom, found that falling asleep in his alcove was difficult. He looked down on River Street briefly, and from his hot bed listened to the *música norteña* booming out of the pool hall until it fell silent. Restless, he went downstairs to watch television, but by now two of the three stations had signed off, and a movie on the third didn't seem compelling. The night air was heavy and still as he stood briefly on the front porch and looked around. The streets were totally deserted. There was no movement except intermittent neon signs on a few businesses and an occasional flash of lightning, far away and low, that produced no thunder, while beyond City Hall a parked police car generated a revolving red beam that splashed the surrounding buildings sequentially with each circuit.

Marcus went back inside and upstairs to the bathroom, where, from its window, the backyard was visible in the light from the city. At that moment Jimmy's car pulled up and parked just beyond the cooling tower for the air conditioners. He jumped out, and a girl slid out the driver's door behind him.

It slowly dawned on Marcus who the girl was after he remembered Jimmy's occasional remarks about her. Jimmy had a singular talent for locking on to a girl once he knew a name and for getting a date, to the complete amazement of all, with successes ranging from the bus-station waitress to the wealthy and educated. He casually enlisted the aid of a female he somehow met at the police station, and she willingly and often supplied the names associated with the license plates of cars bearing likely prospects. Jimmy proceeded from there. He had no qualms about calling any girl, and those who signed the funeral register were innocently unaware of his examination and exploitation of this resource until he made follow-up calls and showed up at their doors, overdressed in a dark flannel suit that he thought added importance to his thin frame. His liberal use of the funeral home name then became a helpful personal reference.

It was no surprise that Jimmy was with the girl whose hand he held now as he took her through the garage to the back chapel downstairs. She had been identified inadvertently in a newspaper article regarding a rape case, and her name, already familiar in the high school, was circulated in even more detailed sexual gossip now among the boys in the college and elsewhere as a girl who had liberally rewarded boys with her favors. All things stemmed from an unbelievably ill-fated night when she had an escapade with three young men, one a former friend of Marcus. The trial involving her seized Guadalupe City and revealed again to its citizens that Mexicans were not white.

A well-known football player in high school, Daniel Martinez, drove with his two buddies, Cantu and Contreras, out of Riverside Park to the place where the road approached and ran just parallel to The River. Marcus had traveled this way many times and watched children playing and adults splashing in the shallow water just off a flat, sandy bank. Swimming in the clean water was a common joy in some of the deeper spots. The site was popular with high school students as a place to go with girls at night or to play hooky during the school day. The trial brought out, and the newspaper accounts embellished, the details of many unfortunate events, fictional, attorney-inspired, or otherwise, and townspeople's imaginations frequently filled in where data were missing. The three boys had been driving around in the night with a case of beer, looking for lovers in the cars parked along the back roads. The sport in doing this came from approaching a car with your headlights off, then turning on the lights with a hoot and a holler while driving past. The startled couple, or couples, usually leaped up in fear or anger, or both, and their reaction was the intruders' reward. Though never fully substantiated, reports of irate lovers taking a shot or two at their tormentors gave the game a little added excitement.

Martinez and his friends spotted a car parked just off the road, and pulled their stealthy trick. The car was empty. Convinced that the lovers had gone down to the water, and fortified with enough beer to act on their suspicions, the three guys scrambled down the bank to have a look. From the moment of this decision, the courses of their lives, their futures and aspirations, and the good, soul-fed dreams held by their families for them were changed by a most egregious series of events.

Two girls, one of whom had just disappeared downstairs with Jimmy, were swimming. It was a bright night with sufficient moonlight to make out the specifics of the girls' semi-nakedness. The boys walked down and started talking to them. What happened next is known only to the five people involved, and the accuracy of those memories was likely distorted by others' manipulations. The prosecutor made the following case: the boys joked with the girls a while and coaxed them out of the water. The girls put their dresses on over their wet underwear, and the five of them sat on a quilt spread on the grass just above the waterline. They finished the beer and in some fashion of sharing, began kissing, with, the prosecution admitted, no resistance. The activity became more passionate, and both girls eventually had their dresses up around their waists and open at the top. One of the boys, Cantu, pulled his pants off and attempted to enter the girl whom Jimmy was probably undressing downstairs at that very moment. Martinez pushed him off, the prosecutor said, because he was the leader and wanted to be first. The debate apparently revived the girls who, cooled off or frightened, began to rearrange their clothes, saying, "We have to go."

The prosecutor contended further that the boys would have none of it, and the girls testified that they were trying to get up when they were pushed back down. Cantu held Jimmy's girl, she being stocky and a little tougher, and Martinez mounted her. It was over quickly and his companion took his place. The other couple, Contreras and the unknown girl, finished, and the five of them—without speaking, it was said—walked back to the cars. The next day the sheriff's department picked the Mexicans up, and their prison lives began.

The youths told a different story of their encounter with the swimmers. They had found the girls splashing and giggling and called out to them. Neither group knew the other because the girls were about three years younger. With little modesty, the girls stepped from the water and walked toward the quilt, pulled on their dresses and drank the proffered cans of beer. Soon, casual kissing began, with the girls taking the lead, kissing one boy and then another in no particular order. In a little while, according to the boys, the girls were supine, encouraging the boys with gestures. Cantu stripped his pants down and tried to enter Jimmy's girl, but Martinez pushed him off, saying in Spanish that he didn't have a rubber and that they had better not try it because the girls were so young and white. The Mexicans argued among themselves, and the girls, not understanding the language or the purpose of the discussion, sat up. They were curious and perhaps a little frightened—nobody knows—but they did nothing more than watch. Jimmy's girl said, "We have to go," but did not get up. The defense attorney argued that the statement, "We have to go," referred to the need to void—or, as he said, "pass water"—and was not intended to indicate sexual reluctance on the part of the girls.

Fondling and kissing, the five began again, and Martinez first, Cantu second, entered Jimmy's girl, and Contreras coupled with the second young woman, all within a few minutes. They dressed and went back to the cars, and someone suggested that they ride around for a while. Jimmy's girl, conceivably displaying her affectionate feelings, sat near Martinez, who drove, and the other two boys sat in the back on either side of the second girl. The girls testified that the boys were quiet and content, their energies dissipated. After an hour or so, Martinez drove back to the girls' car, still parked on the road beyond the park. The second girl and Contreras climbed out. Martinez, Jimmy's girl, and Cantu, now in the front seat, drove around town, twin tailpipes roaring, and witnesses said they saw a woman's underwear flying from the radio aerial.

Around midnight, Martinez and Cantu took Jimmy's girl home. She, a deputy sheriff's daughter, had been seen in the car with the two Mexicans by a patrolman who knew the deputy's family. The noise of the car, especially the droning of the twin mufflers, had attracted his attention. It was by accident that the father later heard of the trophy on the boys' antenna. As he sat in the toilet stall just before going off duty, the deputy heard that same patrolmen joking about the story making the rounds in the station just now, that two Mexican boys were seen driving with carefree audacity around town. "They had a pair of girl's drawers on the antenna," the patrolman said. Now, after the night shift ended, as the deputy had breakfast before going home, one of the group at the table, a policeman known for openly expressing his dislike of Mexicans who dated white girls, purposefully mentioned that the deputy's daughter was riding around town with two boys, whom he didn't identify as Mexican, "making a lot of racket." The deputy sheriff put the information from the unseen informants in the washroom together with the latter statement. He flew home, woke the sleeping girl, and demanded an account from her of the night's events. Charges of rape against the three boys were filed that same day by both girls.

A few months later, the trial began, and witnesses verified that the girls were generally known as promiscuous, and the boys were acknowledged to be good citizens, one a football player with the support of the team and many of the student body. The girls insisted that sexual intercourse had taken place by force, and the defense insisted that the crime, if any had occurred, was intercourse with a consenting minor.

The jury said rape, not statutory rape, and the judge said twenty years each, and the three boys disappeared from Guadalupe City forever. The dispatch of Martinez and Cantu had little effect on Marcus. He barely knew them. The third boy, Contreras, however, was Trine, that very friend who had pedaled Marcus around City Park on the back of his bicycle when they were twelve, with whom he had picked cotton row after row, who had spoken of intimate things and insisted in the burning fields back then that he had conquests of eager Spanish maidens. That same Trine, poor Trine, *pachuco* friend, guilty of consensual sex with a young white girl.

Jimmy was either in the back chapel, where a long couch or the deep, soft carpet could accommodate him and his date, or else he had taken her into the ladies' lounge. Marcus walked to the head of the stairs and listened, but could hear only the knocking of the pendulum clock in the hall. Now he was wondering what was going on, but finally gave up, went to bed, and thought about Contreras and Martinez, the athlete, and Cantu and Jimmy and the girl downstairs. Next morning, Jimmy was buck naked when he ran into the bathroom, which was odd because the night crew always slept in under shorts to hasten their dressing for emergency ambulance runs.

"I didn't get any sleep last night," Jimmy said.

Marcus asked, "Why not?" and pretended to be ignorant of the tryst downstairs.

"Well," he said, "I picked this ol' gal up, and she damn near fucked me to death."

⌒26⌒

His options used up at the junior college, Marcus knew that it was time to move on, and the Air Force recruiter gave him a bus ticket to San Antonio for a navigator's test. Sunday night was quiet in the deserted downtown's YMCA, and around him were the strewn ions, the wanderers, like himself, lying and sitting on the bunks, looking around. On the bunk parallel to his, a thin chain-smoker with a wedding ring stared at the floor, and across the aisle a late teenager with a round, sad face kept giving Marcus looks as if in appeal to a wiser one who had some special advice for him. The married man spoke, "This is the first time in a long time that I've spent the night without my wife."

"Oh, yeah," Marcus answered. "What are you here for?"

"I'm going into the Army tomorrow."

He continued to smoke and said nothing else. Marcus tried to sleep, but the motions and movements of men coming in from the street and rattling their possessions as they settled in kept him awake, sufficiently conscious to realize that he was catching something and had a fever that made his ears ring and the bed move slightly with every heartbeat, and his brief naps contained frustrating and baroque dreams in which he tried to add large columns of numbers or write telephone messages requesting an ambulance, only to make mistakes and have to start over. The distorted time of that night finally passed, and before the doors were unlocked at the recruiting station, he was there.

The examiner gave him instructions and added, to be helpful, that he did not need to answer all one hundred questions, recommending that he choose fifty because the grading was based on the fraction correctly answered over the number attempted and not on the total. Marcus did as he was told and took a seat in the corridor to wait for the results with a certain amount of confidence in his ability. After all, he thought, he had taken the exams to get into West Point that summer after high school graduation and had the highest score in his group in Guadalupe City and was named the primary nominee for an appointment. With the congratulatory telegrams from Senator Johnson and Senator Yarbrough, it was an exciting time for a seventeen-year-old, first, to get telegrams delivered to his door, and then to get them from far-off Washington. He had worried about passing the physical, and especially the vision test, and probably among the many regrettable missteps in the series, had gone to an optometrist who told him that drinking milk and Cokes was giving him pimples and that his vision was about 20/30 or 20/40, so he might not get into West Point. Marcus believed him, a little, for West Point was a place where, he believed, men had to have perfect 20/20 eyesight and were helped to get in by having smooth, white skin; by knowing how to dance; by belonging to military and comfortably well-off families.

Then the father boasted to people on the street and at his night watchman's job that "his boy" was going to West Point. Immediately, Marcus wrote letters to Senator Johnson and to Senator Yarbrough, Washington, District of Columbia, on notebook paper, to say that he was withdrawing from the candidacy for an appointment to the United States Military Academy. He would never do anything that might possibly acknowledge any link to his father or improve his father's stature. Besides, he would rather dream about the extraordinary rewards of attending West Point than risking getting in, failing to do so, and having a dream die.

He wasn't out of Guadalupe City yet, though, but he knew he was smart, and he thought of those impressive telegrams and shaky dreams as he sat in the hallway, staring at the pictures of proud Air Force officers and their jets.

A sergeant called for Marcus Reel. In the recruiter's office, he was told that he had failed the test. Stunned, Marcus could only answer that he didn't feel well that morning, anyhow. He wouldn't be going to the navigator's school; he would be going back to Guadalupe City. Was there some mistake? Was his answer sheet somehow applied to another's name? It didn't seem right.

Marcus grappled with his defeat as he walked back to the Greyhound station. He felt profoundly unworthy. He remembered the all-but-abandoned home of an ambulance patient he had once picked up. In that sorry and neglected yard, beautiful daffodils bloomed, as they did yearly, even for the laziest and most indifferent people who lived in that house. They didn't seem to deserve such a free blessing. They didn't work for it, but were given it, invariably. Marcus told himself, though, that he personally had always absorbed nature and appreciated beauty. He deserved a better outcome.

The deep gloom of the first leg of the bus ride back to Guadalupe City was made worse by the loud conversation of the driver with a lady in the seat behind him as he regaled her with his tales of odd things and curious occurrences on his route, turning completely from the road from time to time to face her, charming her with his unusual hazel-colored eyes and a broad, crooked smile, interrupting his animated stories by adjusting his soft, wrinkled cap to tilt it from one side to the other, throttling the noisy diesel down on the curves and effortlessly working the gears up and down the hills. Marcus got off in Gonzales, glad to be free, to wait for the connecting bus and relieved that there was plenty of time to walk to the cemetery to visit his mother's grave, where he knew some comfort must be.

He crossed the park in front of the county courthouse with its customary monument to a Texas patriot, and cut through the square that had the usual collection of pickup trucks and the same pecan buyers and appliance dealers that had been there before, when he was called a boy. He followed the railroad tracks that he knew would lead him to the city cemetery beyond a small settlement of dilapidated sheds and old feed and grain businesses and a few Mexican families with running children outside. The clouds were lower and the sky more overcast now, and the air felt damp and much colder than it was in San Antonio.

He was alone with his mother in the empty cemetery, and every misery that he had ever experienced surfaced. It would have been too obvious and uncomfortably prayerful to kneel at her grave, so he sat back on his heels like a child at play with jacks or marbles and, for the first time ever, wept for her and for himself, and mental pain deeper than any he had seen or felt in the funeral home and at half a thousand interments made the sore throat and thick congestion of his cold seem inconsequential. His life wasn't being watched from above but from here, imbedded in this earth with her infant, and he knew that whatever made his soul function emanated from this piece of ground where she slept beneath the crepe myrtle trees with strangers. *Mama, mama, come up and help me.*

➤ 27 ➤

The three women, one older and bent and two young and very pretty, stood with their backs to the wind. It was overcast, and the unpleasant air caused the hair of the younger women to swirl around their faces. The women's woolen suits, dark and brown, were not unlike the color of the earth incompletely covered by the fake grass near the open, undecorated grave, and clumps of the soil were scattered carelessly about as if the haste to get the burial over with did not allow tidying up. Only the brilliant red carnations atop the simple wooden casket were beautiful. Everything else seemed to be rendered in the monotone of the gray day. The casket disappeared from view and seemed to drop the last foot or so with an unexpected brusqueness, as if the lowering device added some personal anguish to the gentleness of its sad ritual. The minister began to read aloud from his notes and spoke the name of the young man who had grown up across The River. Pain poured from the faces of the three women. Not even the tears on their faces could lessen the beauty of the younger ones.

Marcus had now journeyed through another winter in the funeral home with nights on the streets and roadways with Frank's oft-repeated and cheerful expression as accompaniment: " Only people out this time of the night are burglars and undertakers." In the enclosure of the cars and ambulances, the lights of the dashboard glowing on these trips, all seemed warm and reassuring. Once, the miracle of snowflakes floated down on Guadalupe City, whitening the grass in front of the funeral home and inspiring Frank's brother, who liked so much to talk about the weather, to become even more animated.

Now springtime arrived again with its sweet green smells outside and warm-weather bird activity in the shrubs alongside the banister of the front gallery and among the palm fronds, where a new neighborhood of yellow jacket nests was well under construction. This spring was imbedded in permanent memory, which horrendous tragedies are apt to generate, by a devastating crash in the April morning fog at the highway intersection with the road from the chemical plant where four men in one car had just finished their night shift. They were in four caskets at last: one in the large chapel, one in the small chapel, one in the preparation room, and one in the hall outside of the bedrooms.

Marcus lay in bed, weary, drifting, floating away from that grief-filled day. He heard faint intestinal growls coincident with the respiration of one of the profoundly tired men, Hank or Jimmy or even Frank in the next room. Marcus had read once about African elephants. The author said that they communicated through some kind of rumbling stomach sounds as they fed. African elephants emitting noises, maybe like those of the funeral-home workers now asleep, retired with silent petitions, having asked for a quiet night. African men. *King Solomon's Mines.* Saw it in the fifth grade. Tall, thin, graceful natives with feminine hands. Tall and thin like himself. Willie a lot shorter, light-skinned, thicker. African elephants fanning their ears. Then nothing.

His second summer in the funeral home was at hand, passing, accelerating toward some new place. Reel always knew that he had to get away and keep away from his early life, had to put some distance between then and now. His unfortunate reference to that past time was, he envisioned, those who still endured their sessile lives across The River. This meant that any small acts—like eating in a nice restaurant with linen napkins and small portions, wearing a suit, driving the Cadillacs in the funeral procession— were all evidence of his escape and confirmation of his special status. At any moment he could analyze his situation and think of his previous existence and of the people who had not moved up or out, had not read and learned great words and magnificent things. Of course, his small achievements were trivial because they were measured against such pitiful standards. He spoke to Willie about it.

"You don't think that you deserve better things, Slim," Willie answered. "Maybe you ought to try and let go. Don't hold back. Use up what you got. Don't save it, spend it. I know a guy who owns a brand new Chevrolet, and he put those damn clear plastic seat covers in it. They're hot. You stick to them. What's the point of saving the factory seat covers anyhow?"

"Willie, you are a wise man," Marcus responded, "How did you learn these things? I know you didn't go out there to junior college."

"No, but I did graduate from high school."

"Which one?"

"Gross High."

"I loved the Gross High Bumblebees," Marcus said, "especially the cheerleaders. They could crack gum so loud that you could practically hear them up in the stands. I can still remember them out there. 'Watermelon, watermelon, watermelon rind. Bumblebees, Bumblebees, hold that line!' They say that one of the players, a guy named Rufus, was twenty-six years old. That was some football team."

And so Marcus recognized now, more than ever, how he had grappled with his internal convictions that he wouldn't have much in his life, how he had chosen elusive objectives that he reached for but never grasped. It was like the times in his young life that he was conscripted to rush into the chicken house and grab and stuff the chickens into crates, only to find that because he hadn't selected a fixed target, each escaped, flapping and running. The only result was he had inhaled the waste and flying dust that smelled of feathers and droppings, yet another frustration birthed by the long-ago sadness and deprivation that he had been helpless to prevent.

The funeral home changed all of that. Marcus rooted there in the cool, dark rooms among good mentors who gave him father-like guidance and respectful support. Almost as a fulfillment of a Darwinian prophesy, he, the species Marcus Reel, had radiated into a new environment, adapted, survived, even prevailed. That was his triumph.

He saw enormous suffering, death, wasted lives that ended in nothing, and difficulties far beyond anything he would ever imagine. Living or dying could depend on such small margins of time or distance. Of course, he was overextended, trying to keep the job going, getting up for ambulance calls, missing classes, behaving inconsistently sometimes, becoming marginally psychotic. He presented a face to the world that was, for some observers, dark and indifferent, a man so absorbed in his melancholy and sometimes-pitiable life that even a small joy required enormous exertion. His determination to make himself feel better about his life was a struggling façade for the most part, but he accepted it unconditionally because he thought that adversity made him intense and that it was good to hurt for that reason alone.

He didn't need psychotherapy. He only needed for more things to change in his favor.

Done now and knowing he needed something next, Marcus went to the post office and located the draft board. "Will I be drafted soon?" he asked, after giving his name. A gray-haired lady, well into her sixties, looked at him and wordlessly followed a list with her finger, keeping the folder tilted so she alone could view it.

"Possibly, about six months from now," she answered.

That wouldn't do.

"Is there anything I can do to get into the Army sooner?"

"You can join."

"But that's three years," Marcus said.

"Well, you can go for six months of active duty, what's called an RFA, then spend five and a half years in the reserves, right here at home in Guadalupe City."

That wouldn't do either. Who would want to be back here in only six months?

"Or," she finally released him, "you can waive your rights and volunteer for the next draft call, about two months from now. What happens is that you have a right not to be drafted until you are twenty and a half, and you can waive those rights and go now at age twenty."

"*That's* what I want to do."

She pulled a form from a file drawer and, after getting a little information from him, took his signature; his civilian days at the funeral home were ending. Rhapsodizing and romanticizing in his mind, the strongest of martial urges welled up now, and he had dreams of uniforms, honor and courage, of German strength and German discipline, a face to the enemy. He would soldier, he had to; he must pass from Guadalupe City into the Army. The need to be one of its hard-bodied warriors in faraway lands was unimaginably, unquestionably necessary.

The walk back to the Texas Star Café was slow and mindless as Marcus, pensive, was bound by the enormity of the thought that his transport from one life to another would be good for him somehow. In his mind, he had a conversation with Doris. It was she to whom he would first release his news and she who made his lips move now without a sound as he walked along Main Street. Doris received the news of his decision with a grin. "I can't talk now," she said as she hurried away, "but we're having a birthday party for Shirley on Friday night after we close. Come over then."

In the community of the funeral home, Para, Willie, McCullough, everyone reinforced his decision. These old men knew that young men joined the Army. They were naturally jingoistic, and Marcus appreciated it.

Doris' homely sister, Shirley, laughed and celebrated, and whiskey and Coke had fortified the merriment when Marcus tapped on the locked front door of the café. Shirley's husband sat next to her in the booth, comely Doris beside Marcus, closer than ever. Her hand rested on his leg, up high, the most sexual touch he had ever felt from a white woman, nothing like the handling he had paid for in Villa Acuna. He was erect and self-conscious. Shirley held a gift pair of pink panties at her waist, the crotch at her own, and thrust her pelvis forward in simulation. The whiskey anesthetized Marcus. He had to get back to work. Doris kissed him, mouth open, at the door. He could hardly walk back to the home. He knew that he loved her, and she loved him.

Marcus was ready to leave the funeral home seven weeks later and go, his clothing having been packed in an aluminum suitcase that he found in an Army-Navy surplus store. Para gripped his hand and nodded without speaking. Dietz stayed at home with some common ailment of old age. Hank said, "Don't catch anything, Slim." Jack and Arthur smiled broadly and wished him luck. Jimmy mentioned needles and shots. "I'll sure miss you, Slim," he said. Marcus could never return such intimacy and could not tell any of them how he deeply would miss them all, that there was sadness in leaving home. He would stop by when he got leave, he promised.

Out back, he walked up behind Willie, sitting in the tree-shaded yard, his back to the doorway of the garage. "So long, Willie."

Willie rose from the lawn chair, removed his Borsalino hat, a spontaneous gesture of respect and humility, more profound than anything Marcus had ever experienced. It was an instantly sad and moving moment because Marcus didn't think that he had any superior status over Willie. He didn't want things to happen that way. To him, Willie was a friend who even ordered him around occasionally, not a Negro. He reached for Willie's hand and made the closest move toward a hug that he had ever offered another man. He grasped Willie by the forearm, between the wrist and elbow, and Willie, eyes glistening, mouth pinched, did the same. "So long, Slim. Good luck."

Now he was in the bus from Guadalupe City, which, after a transfer in the town where his mother lay, would take him to San Antonio. He stared at the passing roadside without seeing, thought of Willie, how he would miss his friend and confidant, and of Willie's humble goodbye. Thick sadness made Marcus swallow hard and breathe deeply. Had Willie, in his wisdom, seen a burgeoning adult dignity, a development of maturity that Marcus could not perceive in himself during those two years? Yes, that was it. Willie had provided approbation and acknowledgement of Marcus' growth when the others in the funeral home had not. Did Marcus evoke a different standard of behavior, suddenly submissive, from this Negro because he was a white man? That couldn't be it. He missed Willie.

His mind pictured Doris, and a warm heat seemed to suffuse his chest, ardor replacing the emptiness a little. He wished again for the smoke-tasting kiss she had given him in the doorway of the Texas Star just the other month, and he knew he must see her, with husband or not, as soon as his Army let him. He remembered her jocund laugh when he asked if she could make him a *chalupa*, and she said she didn't know how because she didn't know what it was, then proceeded to bring him the usual bowl of greasy chili and crackers. He needed to love and be loved before something bad could happen like it had to those young men he had seen buried too soon. She, he reasoned at that moment, may be the one to hold him eventually, hopefully sexually, some day.

In the bus terminal after the first leg, Marcus sat in the pale-green waiting room near the "Whites Only" water fountain and looked to the west, toward his mother. He did not visit her, but her presence in that same town made him think about the early years when she was real and they lived on The Farm that was only seven miles away.

A cinema of that other life merged with the present now in the frame of the next bus window as if it were a screen. He remembered Red Ryder and Little Beaver and B.O. Plenty and Sparkle, the heat of too-small shoes that were worn only once each week on Sunday morning, and the time Bill Cady dropped his molasses can and it popped open, and his few biscuits rolled away to be thrown and crumbled by older kids as Bill cried because that was all he had to eat. Slipping past were memories of an old man who jacked up a Model A, which he had affectionately christened "Strawberry Roan," to power a screaming saw blade off the rear wheel when he cut firewood and of an overnight bus that hit a blackjack oak when the driver fell asleep one foggy dawn and the family came upon the wreck where people lay with legs snapped at grotesque angles, and the moans and crying of the shocked and injured continued, and still no help arrived. Marcus would not make another red rubber slingshot as the images of the War softened and bleached away and that wartime red rubber disappeared forever. *Goodbye, Mama.*

The big, wallowing Greyhound continued on its way, and Marcus stared up at the universe, pure and blue, cumulus clouds stretching on and on in towering clumps. The physics of the sky absorbed him, captured him in a kind of torpid reverie. Beyond these great white vapors he imagined infinity and beyond, but these were here and near, and silently shadowed the pasture landscapes, those drowsy nodding oil pumps and fields of sunflowers looking patiently to the east, sweating black men hauling watermelons to towns with German names and Mexican names, distant gulf sides beyond Guadalupe City, and faraway African elephants with grumbling bowel sounds.

Then, there, on the horizon, was the radio-TV antenna on the tallest building in the city.

The recruits sat at tables across from each other and took the written exams. The tests were too easy, and not even the desultory looks from a young, fat kid with an acne-studded face opposite him could keep Marcus from scoring far higher than the others. All stood, naked men in a line, their wallets, coins, and keys in bags hanging around their necks. They were ordered to move from station to station, examined, screened, foreskin pulled back, venipunctured, measured, ordered to move again, fingerprinted, palpated, weighed, and finally brought before a doctor, the last station.

"You have scoliosis. That means your spine is crooked," he said looking at his pad, writing. "You didn't pass the physical."

Marcus had never counted on this horror. A wave of weak sickness washed through him. "But you have to take me," he cried. "I have no place to go."

The doctor sighed and shook his head, acknowledging the words he doubtless had heard from many, many others. Watching him intently, he asked, "Does your back bother you?"

"No," Marcus lied. "I never have any trouble." The good doctor's magnanimous self shone through and he modified the health record, rescued yet another impoverished boy.

Marcus now sat above the wing, watching the engines cranking and the white exhaust smoke surrounding them, the vibrations and shaking and backfiring, then acceleration to speeds beyond his comprehension and the air rushing by as the sun set on San Antonio's houses, growing smaller below. He had crossed The River. He was away. Lifted free. Down, down there in Guadalupe City, a final, grinding, unspeakable loss, but unknown to him. Doris, only twenty-three, died from a cerebral hemorrhage that came out of nowhere. The funeral home buried her in Catholic Cemetery Number Two.